Lainy Malkani is  Indo-Caribbean root and presenter of the which is a series of interviews designed to bring the stories of unsung heroes to life. Lainy has written for the British Library, the Commonwealth and the BBC. She says:

'*Our cultures give us room to breathe in a fast-changing world - and it is our duty to capture their essence for future generations.*'

Lainy is married with two children and lives in north-west London. Her cross-cultural roots - from Britain, India and the Caribbean - have been a great source of inspiration for her work, both as a writer and as a journalist.

Visit *www.socialhistoryhub.com*

Sugar, Sugar

Bitter-sweet Tales of Indian
Migrant Workers

LAINY MALKANI

hope**road** : London

HopeRoad Publishing Ltd
PO Box 55544
Exhibition Road
SW7 2DB

First published in Great Britain by HopeRoad 2017

Supported using public funding by

ARTS COUNCIL ENGLAND

ISBN 978-1-908446-60-2

eISBN 978-1-908446-66-4

www.hoperoadpublishing.com

Typeset in Perpetua 14 pt

Printed and bound by TJ International Ltd, Padstow, Cornwall, UK

For my mother

CONTENTS

FOREWORD

By Sanjeev Bhaskar

It is well known that the Indian diaspora has spread far and wide across the world. The success of these communities, particularly in the UK, Canada and the US, has brought forth fine writing about the journeys and experiences of those who travelled, settled and then prospered in their new homes. Many of these stories relate to the people who travelled post-Partition in 1947. These families and individuals journeyed as free men and women, mainly as economic migrants and at the invitation of their new countries, seeking to bolster their own economies.

However, their stories have masked the tales of those who were coerced to journey as indentured labour to places that, at the time, were far less hospitable than they are today. The Caribbean, particularly Trinidad and Tobago, Guyana, Fiji, Mauritius and South Africa all saw large numbers of Indian workers brought to work on the land, mainly as labourers. These people remained as indentured labour pretty much for the duration of the Empire, finding partners, raising families and making these countries their home; generations later, their descendants are part of the fabric, culture and identity of these independent nations.

In this collection, Lainy Malkani shines a light on those 'less travelled' stories and wonderfully weaves them together using 'sugar' as the connecting thread. Her tales encompass the wrench of being separated from one's homeland, the dreams of return, and a desperation to escape - through to the nostalgia, acknowledgement and tribulations of having such a past in one's family history.

Set in tropical lands that today many regard as exotic paradises, Lainy's stories convey the darker emotional hues, the horror and complexities that so many men and women faced - but also the importance of connection, belonging and kinship.

Sugar may never taste quite the same again . . .

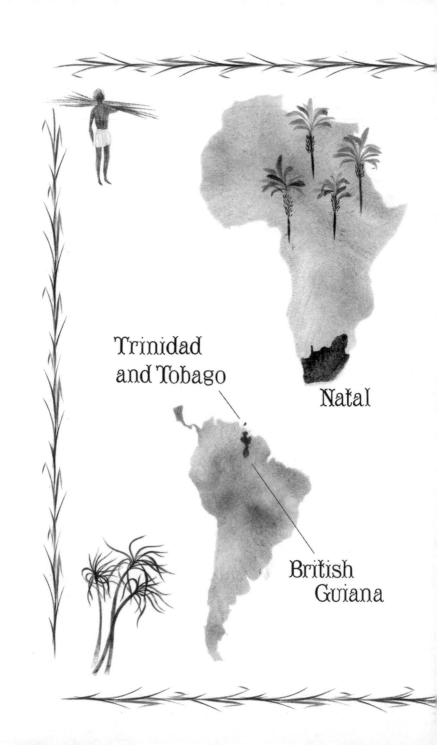

Trinidad
and Tobago

Natal

British
Guiana

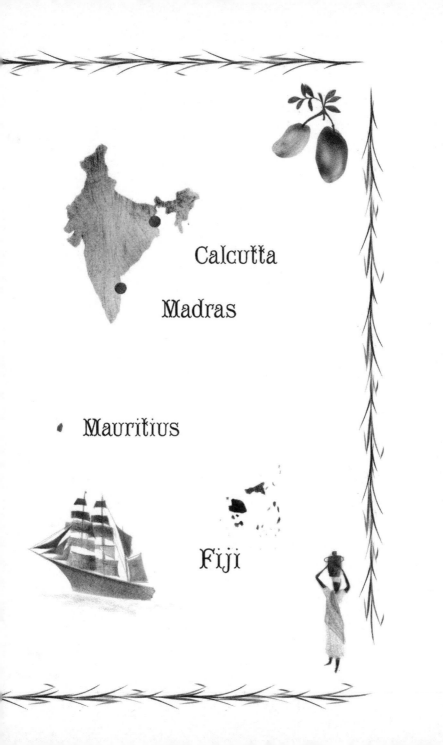

Calcutta

Madras

Mauritius

Fiji

The Berbice Chair

Finsbury Park, North London, 1986

LOT NO. 33 WAS a beautiful wicker chair. Alicia felt attracted to it the moment she saw it. It was love at first sight. The chair had an elegant sloping back, a bit like a modern reclining chair, and a long seat - so that when you sat in it, your body slid down into a half-sleeping position. The wicker was woven in diamond shapes and had a tinge of yellow, like hay; the armrests, made of teak, cradled your arms from the elbow to the fingertips.

Best of all were two discreet hinges below the armrests where two planks, rather like flat boat oars, were attached; they could be released and pulled forward to extend the arms. It was this part of the chair that was most interesting to Alicia, because when you swung out the oars you could also make them meet in the middle, forming a bridge where the sitter could rest their legs and watch the world go by.

It was not too expensive either. On the contrary, there were only two other buyers interested in the chair, and so as to waste no time, Alicia immediately bid a full forty pounds even though, as she found out later, her main rival had only intended to pay a straight twenty.

Still, she told herself that she had a bargain and that if she could sell it for fifty, she would have done all right. Alicia's second-hand shop on the Stroud Green Road had existed at number 72 for over fifty years, and during that time she had seen a thousand clients come and go. In the beginning, they were mainly the unemployed or poor immigrants - and it pleased her to think that the items she sold were helpful to others. Everything was reasonably priced and was mostly going to a good home.

As time moved on, she began to see a new type of client. They had a little more money in their pockets; sometimes ate out in the Turkish restaurant three doors down; shopped less in the greengrocers and more in the supermarkets, where the price was sometimes double for the same carrots and greens. They started to call Alicia's stock *vintage* and demanded more and more curious and exotic things to buy.

Once, she bought an African rosewood mask in West Green Road for ten pounds and sold it in her shop for twenty, although one of her suppliers said that he could have got it for a fiver. Soon, Alicia found that she was becoming more, how shall we say, 'au fait' with the goods that she sold. A set of silver spoons from Hampstead, owned by some Lady or other, could push up the price. On the other hand, a door knocker from the home of a mass murderer could fetch three times what she asked. That is why she began to go to auctions; after all, any good antiques dealer, as she now called herself, should surely know their pieces and what they were worth on the open market. But the story of the chair eluded her.

'Sometimes, something just pulls at your heart-strings,' she told a customer looking for French perfume bottles. He nodded politely and pointed to a deep purple glass bottle with a delicate lid that had a thin gold ring etched around the rim. His eyes glowed when he held it up to the light.

'Is that what they call instinct?' she continued. 'You don't know why and you don't care - you just have a feeling that you have got to have it.'

However, things did not go quite as smoothly as she had anticipated once she brought the chair home. She placed it in the shop window, believing that it would be an attraction for passing trade, but people walked straight past the chair, just ignoring it, not stopping even to admire its beauty. There was one man - shy, perhaps - who walked past three times in a row. The first on his way to somewhere, the second as if he were on his way back, and the third . . . well, back again. He didn't stop, just looked, looked and looked again. He was Indian, no longer young, and not quite like the other Indians she was used to. She overheard him greeting someone and noticed that he had a West Indian accent. He was stylish, she thought, with his slicked-back hair, but in an awkward sort of way.

Perplexed, she stood outside the shop and tried to see the chair through the eyes of passers-by. She cleaned the glass inside and out, polished the wooden arms and pulled out the oars to display them, but still not a single customer even came in to enquire about it.

As summer approached, she put it outside in the courtyard and invited people to take a seat, but they did not stop.

Four weeks passed and still the chair was not sold. So, Alicia decided to up her game. She put the chair back in the window, and placed a large floor lamp on one side of it. The lampstand matched the teak, and the green hexagonal lampshade with tassels around the edge complemented the chair. It gave it a colonial look, which was in fashion. On the other side, she set a small round dark wood coffee table. It had white elephant carvings on the tabletop and down each of the four legs. At the back of the chair, she positioned a lush green palm tree in a copper pot and spread out the palms so that they dangled lazily - like a scene from the tropics - over the top.

She was gratified when a few passers-by did stop by the window to have a look at the new arrangement, and when a tall, clean-shaven man with a leather satchel slung over his shoulder entered the shop, she stood up from behind her desk expectantly and led him to the chair.

'Feel how smooth the arms are,' she said, running her fingers along the grain. She invited him to do the same, but as it turned out, and much to Alicia's disappointment, he wanted to buy the lamp. So now she found herself twenty pounds richer but still with no sale of the chair.

By September, Alicia decided it was time for another new approach. She replaced the floor lamp with a table lamp and rummaged around at the back of the shop, digging out three long pinewood louvre doors. She painted each one in a dark wood stain and then went to see the manager of the hardware store next door. She tumbled through boxes of nails and screws and eyed the hammers and drills fastened on the wall. The manager was already serving a dusty, tired builder with paint splashes on his blue overalls. He looked up and winked at her as she stood patiently by the plungers for his attention. He was Cypriot, as she recalled, and on quiet days he would bring her slices of warm baklava bathed in rose-flavoured honey.

They discussed her plans for a few moments before she bought nine gold hinges and a slim screwdriver with a blue translucent handle. She fastened the hinges to the louvre doors and out of nothing had created a stylish divider which she placed at the rear of the chair behind the palm tree.

She then stood back and admired her handiwork - but felt there was still something missing. On the corner of Stroud Green Road, not five minutes' walk from The Emporium, as she now called her business, was a junk shop. It looked tatty from the outside but inside was an Aladdin's Cave of dusty tables and mirrors and odds and ends. Looking around, she wondered why the owner thought that he would be able to sell a naked mannequin with dark kohl eyes and one hand missing, but she was not there to criticise.

She spoke for a short while with the manager, a rotund young man who smelled of beef burgers, and was shown to the corner of the room where there was a pile of rugs. She flipped them over one at a time and chose her favourite, admiring its colours and elaborate patterns, and then bartered him down to half the asking price. She added two pounds for delivery and he rolled it up, tied a rope around its centre, and carried it on his shoulder down the street to her shop. With a toothy smile, she thanked him.

After the man had gone, Alicia unravelled the rug. It was the colour of autumn leaves, dappled with auburn diamond shapes that spread out from the middle like a star. Opening it out on the floor, she pulled at the white tassels on the circular edge to free them, and was pleased with the result.

As evening approached, she switched on the lamp and watered the palm. Weary from her day's hard work, she slipped off her shoes and eased herself down into the chair, dusting off her grubby denim jeans before resting her legs over the oars. Cars and buses floated past her window. She waved to Daphne, an old school friend who worked in the library on Woodstock Road. It was the kind of languid wave that the Queen gives to her subjects from the balcony at Buckingham Palace. They giggled at each other like naughty children in the classroom.

There Alicia sat until the Indian man whom she had seen all those weeks ago reappeared. Once again, he walked past the shop three times. Today he wore a Gibson waistcoat and tie, she noted, and winkle-picker shoes. When he passed for the third time, Alicia thought that he would disappear just as he had done before, but he didn't. Instead, he stopped and rapped on the window.

'How much for the chair?' he shouted through the glass.

Startled, she jumped up and went to open the door. 'Can I help you?' she asked. Then: 'Oh, excuse me, I'm forgetting my manners. Come in, come in.'

The man's tone was as raw as he was rude.

'I don't have time to waste, lady. How much for the chair?' he repeated, without the hint of a smile.

Taken aback, Alicia scanned his face. He looked like Elvis might have done, had he lived. He had the same greased-back hair, perhaps a little longer than before, high cheekbones and a long thin nose that flattened out slightly at the tip. Alicia fixed her eyes on a series of lines on his forehead. They looked like a music sheet that the local children bought from the guitar shop near to Ferme Park Road.

'There is no money kept on the premises,' she said, holding her hands up as though he had a gun. Seeing this, his mood changed and he spoke in a calmer voice.

'Look, I am not here to rob you,' he said. 'Please - put your hands down.'

Alicia did as she was told. Shivering as though she had stepped on to the street in her pyjamas, she wrapped her cardigan close around her body and sat down behind her desk. The street lights came on outside and she looked out of the window, hoping to see someone she knew on the other side.

'I'll give you thirty pounds for it,' the man said impatiently.

'No, no way.' She shook her head. 'For that much I'll sit on it all day and night myself. What do you want it for?'

'I want to chop it up for firewood,' he said sternly.

'You can't destroy something as beautiful as that!' she said, outraged. She glided over to the chair and pushed aside the palm leaves. 'Look at how they cradle your arms,' she said, running her fingers along the grain of the armrests as she had done many times before.

She heard the click of his heels behind her.

'Lady,' the man said, his voice tighter now, 'this chair is a Berbice chair, and I am from Berbice - and you can't tell me it's a beautiful chair because I already know what beauty is - and this is not it!'

Alicia detected a tremor in the man's voice. She dragged over a barstool and coaxed him to take a seat.

'What is this chair to you?' she asked outright.

'It's anger. Terror, sometimes, and sadness - a lot of sadness.' The man ran a hand through his hair. 'Nightmares, fires, the sickly-sweet smell of burning sugar, me pulling the mules along the side of the canal, clearing out the stables, riding horses, racing horses, my mother crying, my father fighting.' He released a shuddering breath.

'Oh,' Alicia said, wondering if the price should rise or fall. 'In that case, why do you want to pay thirty pounds for something that you detest?'

The man swivelled around on the barstool and stopped when he had done a full circle and was facing her again.

'Because, lady,' he bowed his head as if she were royalty, 'you can't get nothing in this country for free.

Back home, if you want a mango, you pick it from the tree; if you want a coconut, you just shimmy up the tree and knock it down. Not here, boy, no way. What's more, I don't want you going around telling everybody that Vincent is a charity case.'

Alicia pretended to look through her books. 'OK,' she said, 'how about I give it to you for thirty-five? We can shake on it with a drink.' Reaching into the drawer at the bottom of her desk, she pulled out two glasses and a bottle of Cuban rum. She placed two coasters on a green-leather-topped table and poured two shots. Switching on the reading lamp, she handed him a glass and then held it back just as he was about to take it.

'Do we have a deal?' she asked, staring at his large black eyes.

'Depends on the quality of the rum,' he replied, and put his hand out again.

She relaxed back in her chair, saying, 'You see, to me it's just a chair, a beautiful piece of furniture.'

Their glasses clinked. He took a sip.

'Tastes good,' he said, tipping the rum in his glass from side to side. Then he went on: 'Seeing you sitting there on the chair, relaxing as though you didn't have a care in the world, took me back to a place I haven't revisited for years.'

His voice cracked as he said: 'She had brown curls too, and they hung around her shoulders in just the same way as yours do. Her skin was white like snow, just like yours. She was fine in her own way, but the manager, her husband, he was a devil.' Vincent knocked back the rum and held out his glass for more.

Alicia looked at the collection of clocks on the wall. It was past closing time. Getting up and going to the shop door, she clicked the latch and flicked the bolt across. The sun had set and heavy clouds streaked with red and pink filled the sky. She saw the Cypriot man from the hardware store cross the pavement and get into his car, and she pulled down the shutter.

'But he is not here now,' she said quietly, taking the glass from her visitor's hand.

'Isn't he? The truth is, he's always around. Somewhere. Lurking up here.' He pointed to his temples, then went on: 'He was a brute with golden hair like an angel. His face was fat like a breadfruit and hard like stone. He was heavy and walked as if he had rocks in his shoes. When that man was around, the whole sugar estate shook! *You!* he would shout down to me from the verandah. *Fetch me my horse, clean up the stables.* And I, like a fool, would run - run down to the stables and scurry around like a helpless fowl in fear of my life. He was a devil all right.'

The man got up and walked over to the chair.

'He had a bell, right here,' he said. He raised a hand to his lips, as though he was smoking a cigar, and took a long puff. 'I can still smell the smoke on his breath,' he muttered, running his fingers along the armrests. Alicia pulled open the drawer at the bottom of the desk and put away the bottle of rum. She wiped the rim of the glasses with tissue and put them away too. She then folded the louvre divider and carried it carefully to the window. Opening it up like a fan, she blocked the view of the chair from the street.

'Follow me, Vincent, and bring the chair with you,' she said, leading him to the garden at the rear of the store.

'Tonight, we're going to have a huge bonfire.'

The Complaint

Durban, 1885

MR KUMAR, a merchant from India, paced up and down behind the counter of his store on Water Street, blowing on a sheet of parchment and waving it in the air. When he was sure that the ink was absolutely dry, he wrapped the item in a white cotton cloth and wedged it between two rice sacks, brushing away the grains that sprinkled on the rough wooden floor.

Sitting propped against the wall next to him, out of sight of the customers, was a young boy. Eyes wide open in sunken sockets, he swayed his head while water trickled down the sides of his gaping mouth. Mr Kumar held a wooden spoon to his lips.

'Here, Khanna, drink some more,' he said to the boy, kneeling beside him. But the poor child was unconscious and could no longer hear him. Mr Kumar sat back on his heels and reached under the counter for an empty rice bag to cover him.

'Sleep, child,' he said, patting him gently on the shoulder. 'For a while at least.'

Opening the back door of the store, the merchant listened to the cool night breeze sending whispers through the trees, and wondered if his family across the Kala Pani in Calcutta still remembered him after all these months.

'I am not the man I used to be,' he whispered back, easing himself into his hammock before closing his weary eyes.

*

When the sun rose the next day, the boy was nowhere to be found and Mr Kumar was glad, because just as he opened the store, the Protector of Immigrants walked in. A boisterous breeze pushed past him, covering the store with a light shower of dust. He tipped his cork hat into his hand as he entered and rested it on the counter. Kicking the dust off his boots, he said casually, 'So - how's business, Mr Kumar?'

Mr Kumar opened the shutters and light flooded the store, which had opened just four months earlier. It was chequered with shelves secured to the walls; here were displayed large bottles of oils and jars of spices. Tattered rice bags laced with string lined the lower shelves, and on the counter, not three feet away, was a set of scales with weights piled beside it.

Mr Kumar wiped the counter and glanced curiously up at the Protector.

'I see the planters have made you a very wealthy man,' the Protector continued, opening a barrel of ghee and drawing his fingers along the thick yellow paste.

Mr Kumar puffed out his chest in a flash of pride.

It was true - he had profited from the new arrivals from India. Since he had opened the store, the demand for rice had increased four-fold in as many months. The planters had developed an insatiable appetite for cheap Indian labour, and their workers all needed to be fed. In recent weeks Mr Kumar had doubled his shipments and had added mustard oil, spices, castor oil, salt and flour to his list of imports. But he had become greedy. The more money that rolled in, the more he wanted. He found that he had started to care less about his customers and more about profits.

Until Khanna came into his life.

'If I am a fortunate man, I am grateful to you all,' he replied graciously.

The Protector was taller than the merchant and had a wide gaping smile that curled the edges of his black moustache. He could have been a handsome man except for a rash of silver scars across his cheeks. Durban's burning sun did not agree with his sensitive pink skin.

Resting one hand on Mr Kumar's shoulder, with his free hand he wiped his sweaty brow.

'It would be a shame to lose it all,' he murmured, tipping back bottles of mustard oil and peering at the labels.

Aware of the disguised threat, Mr Kumar pulled out a handkerchief from his pocket and dabbed at his own brow, glancing surreptitiously at the empty space on the floor where the emaciated boy had first come to plead for help so many nights before. He had promised Khanna's father that he would speak to the Protector about his son's injuries, in the hope that the beatings would stop. Mr Kumar was not one to shirk from his promises, and as a free Indian - and a wealthy merchant to boot - he believed he had some influence. But now that the Protector stood in front of him, he felt his courage slip away.

'Lose it?' he echoed nervously. 'Why would I lose it?'

Before the Protector could answer, a young Madrasi girl called him from the street and pointed towards the sea. Mr Kumar had seen her before; he knew that she worked for the Protector. The *Adventurer*, a large cargo ship from Calcutta, had arrived after three days lost at sea and a stream of people were running down Water Street to meet it. The sun was ferocious in a cloudless blue sky and the Protector winced before grabbing his hat.

Pushed along by the crowd, the merchant followed him and before long was standing at the edge of the sea watching the majestic ship moored out in the bay. It reminded him of his own gruelling journey from India - eight weeks instead of five. 'Enough time for a man to lose hope of ever seeing Mother Earth again,' he whispered to himself.

Sheltering his eyes from the sun, he watched a string of small rowing boats arrive at the shore; the passengers, men in large white turbans, dragged their tired bodies out on to the sand. Business would be good today, Mr Kumar thought as the newcomers were led up the bank to the long, stone-walled depot. The Protector, standing among a group of men dressed in suits and high hats, was there to meet them.

Suddenly, Mr Kumar felt a sharp tug at his shirt sleeve. It was the boy's father.

Before the man could utter a word, the merchant had grabbed him by the arm and hustled him back up the shore into a small hut a short distance from the depot. When Mr Kumar manhandled him, he cowered and held his arms over his head.

'Have you gone mad?' the merchant hissed. He paced the hut, up and down, up and down. 'What if we are seen? I cannot risk everything for you!' he cried out, remembering the Protector's veiled threat earlier that day. 'If I see you hanging around again, even in the shadows, it is you who I will report to the Protector.' He jabbed Khanna's father in the chest.

Mr Kumar was about to slip out of the hut but quickly pulled back, peering in the direction of the barracks. The Indians had formed a line and the Protector was walking along, inspecting them. A second man threw handfuls of white delousing powder over their bodies. Two children in the line clung to their mother's legs; they were almost too weak to stand.

'They say,' the old man quivered, 'that if the beatings continue, my son will die, and many more after him.'

'Do not torment me - there is nothing I can do,' Mr Kumar groaned. Reaching inside his pocket he pulled out a coin, opened the man's hand and pressed it into his palm that was peppered with blisters. As he stared into his sunken eyes in the dim light, for a moment he saw the gaunt face of Khanna staring back at him.

A gavel sounded in the distance, followed by the leathery voice of the Protector, and the line of Indians shunted along. Their term of indenture had begun.

'It can take five years to die in this place,' Khanna's father said. He tugged again at Mr Kumar's sleeve, handing him back the coin. 'Money cannot save you,' he told him. 'In a few days my son will die and I will die too. I will jump into the sea with him in my arms. The 'Kala Pani, the waters of death, will carry us home.'

He stood up, and before leaving the hut, he spoke to the merchant one last time. 'And you, Mr Kumar,' he said, his voice strong now, and dignified. 'What will *you* do?'

*

Mr Kumar studied his long shadow as he walked back to the store, the man's words ringing in his ears. He let himself in and immediately dusted the counter where the Protector's hat had lain earlier that morning; then he lit a low candle. After setting the bottles of mustard oil straight, he locked the door and went behind the counter. Carefully, he leaned the first sack of rice towards himself and pulled out the wrapped sheet of parchment. Taking the candle from the counter, he sat in the same spot where Khanna had collapsed the night before, and began to read.

To the Protector of Immigrants

Sir, the indentured Indians are forced to undergo unimaginable hardships. They do not receive sufficient rations of rice and dhal, oil and salt. The planters hound them, forcing them to rise at 4 a.m. and return to their houses at 5.30 p.m. They work on Sundays, sometimes without water, and dare not complain for fear of being assaulted.

I have been visited three times by these people and have heard terrible accounts of hardship. Mumtaz, a pan boiler, has been badly burned. His hands and back are blistered. I fear that he will not be long in this world. Khanna, a boy of no more than sixteen, is barely able to walk, such is the punishment he receives at the hands of the planters.

I urge you to help them.
Mr Kumar, Water Street

After reading the letter for a second time, Mr Kumar folded the parchment in two and held it over the candle, daring it to catch fire.

'What should I do?' he breathed, waving it closer and closer to the flame. He imagined the Protector, his cheeks red raw where the sun had scorched his face, sitting behind his desk composing a letter of his own:

Dear Sirs,

I write to inform you that the Indians are treated very well in Durban.

They are a diligent people who take pride in their work and are often happy to do copious amounts of overtime when the season demands. They are well fed and live an altogether charmed life in the Colony.

24

Rest assured, you have nothing to fear here,
Signed, The Protector of Immigrants

Mr Kumar slumped down to the floor again. Pulling up his knees until they touched his chin, he snuffed the candle out and sat in the darkness.

*

The following morning, Mr Kumar dressed early. He put on his smartest suit and fiddled nervously with his tie. Brushing flecks of dust from his hat, he set it aside on the counter then pulled back the curtains and opened the shutters. Unexpectedly, he saw the Protector sitting across the street. Despite the yellow haze of the morning light there was no mistaking his long, thin body - perched like a black crow on a wooden bench. He was staring over at the store, puffing on his pipe until swirls of smoke concealed his face. But nothing could conceal his identity.

Mr Kumar stared back at the Protector who, on seeing him open the shutters, had got up and begun to cross the street. His heavy boots kicked at the dry earth, throwing up dust into the air. Wiping his brow with the back of his hand, Mr Kumar stood firm at the door.

The Protector did not wait to be invited in but pushed past him and strode into the store.

'I warned you,' he said, fingering the bottles of mustard oil on the shelf. 'Now where is the letter?'

He glared at Mr Kumar as he held up a bottle and very slowly let it slip from his fingers. It smashed, throwing splinters of glass and yellow oil across the store.

'Oh yes,' he said as another bottle smashed to the floor, 'I saw you down at the docks yesterday with that boy Khanna's father. Curious, I sent my men to fetch him and bring him to the barracks. I didn't realise what a talkative fellow he was, especially when I told him that it was me - not you - who could stop the overseer from punishing his son.'

Mr Kumar dashed towards the Protector and tried to stop him from breaking things. The taller man easily shrugged him off. He swung around and gripped the merchant by the neck, digging his fingers in painfully as he pulled him close. Hot breath smothered Mr Kumar's face.

'The letter,' the Protector demanded.

Hardly able to breathe, Mr Kumar gurgled and shook his head. The Protector released him and shoved him away, then wiped his hand disgustedly on his coat. The merchant watched, horrified, as the Protector began prodding at the sacks of rice behind the counter.

'By the way, did you hear the news? Your little friend Khanna is to be buried today,' he said with a sneer.

Mr Kumar's eyes filled with tears and he lurched once more towards the Protector. Ignoring him, the Protector continued to hunt through the sacks. He quickly found what he was looking for, snatched up the letter and marched out of the door.

Mr Kumar cried out at the top of his voice, but the Protector had gone. Closing the shutters, the merchant sank to the floor and sobbed like a condemned man. He clawed at the dark stain of mustard oil, then got up and ran to the back of the store to fetch a scrubbing brush. Throwing himself down on his knees, he tried desperately to erase the memory of the Protector's destruction. Shards of glass pierced his skin. He scrubbed harder until his knuckles were red raw and he could scrub no longer.

Without thinking, he hurtled out of the store towards the Protector's office and in a rage banged on the front door until it opened. The familiar face of the young Madrasi girl who had called the Protector the day before appeared in the doorway; she was balancing a tray in one hand. She beckoned Mr Kumar inside, pointed to the door marked *Parlour* and then disappeared down the hall.

'Come in, Mr Kumar, we are waiting for you,' the Protector called out from inside the parlour. His voice was light and mischievous.

Mr Kumar gripped the brass door handle to steady his shaking hand. He took a deep breath to prepare himself.

'Come in,' the voice insisted.

Mr Kumar pushed open the door and saw a group of men standing by the window. The Protector was seated behind his desk on the far side of the room. He invited Mr Kumar to sit down, saying, 'You wanted to see me?' and puffed on his pipe.

The smoke caught the back of Mr Kumar's throat and he coughed before replying.

'I am here to bring to your attention the plight of Indian workers who are maltreated every day by devilish planters,' he said bravely.

At that moment, one of the men, neatly dressed in a white suit, broke away from the others at the window and took his seat next to the Protector. He crossed his legs and the two men smiled at each other.

'You were saying?' the Protector said.

*

Mr Kumar was never seen on Water Street again.

After forging the merchant's signature, the Protector had his men frogmarch Mr Kumar down to the docks that same afternoon. In a few weeks' time he would arrive in Mauritius, to be indentured for the next five years to a sugar plantation in Bel Mar.

True to the Protector's threat, the merchant had lost everything.

*

On board the *Gypsy*, Mr Kumar stared out to sea. He thought of Khanna sitting on the floor of his store, his body too weak to move. He licked his lips as he recalled the boy's dry mouth and the wooden spoon dripping water into it. Heavy-hearted, he wished he had been braver, stronger; more willing to stand up to the Protector sooner than he had. Flushed with guilt, his mind shifted towards India and his family back home. They would no longer recognise him. His smart suit, tie and hat had been replaced with a new set of clothes: a loose white shirt, cotton trousers that barely covered his knees, and a turban that weighed him down when he walked.

The glaring midday sun hurt his eyes and he felt his skin tighten as it burned. Turning towards the deck, he noticed a woman standing a few feet away from him, cautiously watching him from under her veil. Although she was a stranger to him, her eyes were the same as Khanna's eyes, the night that the boy came to his store for help. The same eyes he saw in so many of the poor, exhausted Indians who purchased their supplies from his store.

Mr Kumar bowed his head in shame.

'I should have done more,' he said quietly to himself.

Feeling inside the bag of rations that was slung over his shoulder, he found a single coin, the one that Khanna's father had refused to accept the day they met on the shore. He had grabbed it from his jacket pocket just before the Protector's men arrested him, and had held it tightly in his fist all the way down to the docks. It glistened in the sunshine now as he opened his palm to reveal it.

'*Money cannot save you*,' he remembered the boy's father saying.

Mr Kumar slipped the coin back in his bag and walked over to the woman. He smiled gently at her as he took her hand and comforted her. Her trembling fingers wrapped tightly around his as the ship rose and fell over the waves, propelling them towards a new beginning.

Protector of Immigrants to Colonial Secretary 1884:

Colonial Secretary,

I would draw attention to the fact that the Memorial is signed by *M.A. Doorasamy Pilley on behalf of the Indian residents in Natal.*

I cannot conceive in what way M. A. Doorasamy Pilley has obtained the right to explore the wishes of the Indians here. As I point out in the accompanying papers, he has been a resident here since April of last year.

(S.d) L.A. Mason
8.8.84 Protector of Immigrants

———————————

British Library IOR/l/pj/6/145

The Dinner Party

London, 2015

IT WAS ONLY after Suraya had laid the table that she realised she was one plate short. Despite the danger of being late for her own dinner party, she decided to make a quick dash to the local supermarket, which sold everything from cutlery to cake mix and crockery.

Before leaving the flat, Suraya lifted the lid of every pot on the stove to remind herself of the dinner ahead. Each dish had been especially selected to suit her guests. She poked her head close to the pot of yellow dhal still steaming and breathed in deeply, relishing the spicy smells of toasted jeera and garlic. It was her sister Maya's favourite.

Next to the stove was a circular pile of dhal puri wrapped in silver foil. She carefully opened it and broke off a piece of the soft flatbread. The fine granules of ground aromatic spices and yellow split peas inside crumbled onto the kitchen counter. Chewing slowly, Suraya savoured the spicy roasted flavour that she and her young sister Shanti loved so much when they were children. Shanti will be delighted with this tonight, she thought, licking her fingers.

The lamb curry, so soft that the meat fell off the bone, was her mother's idea; and rice for Peter was Maya's. Despite Maya's husband's efforts to scoop up runny dhal with 'the stuffed flatbread', as he called dhal puri, he always ended up licking it off his wrists, putting his wife and the rest of the family off their dinner.

Peter was English and liked exotic food: the brightly coloured 'ball-ah-fire pepper' was one of his favourites. Soaked in vinegar, sugar and salt, it stung the inside of his mouth just the way he liked it. Suraya loved it too, but when she tried to make it at home, the pepper burned her eyes and so she abandoned the idea and bought a bottle from the corner shop instead.

'You were in too much of a hurry, as usual,' her mother scolded her on the phone. 'I told you to wear rubber gloves when you touch the pepper. You could have gone blind.'

Suraya held the phone away from her ear.

The voice nagged on: 'If you had paid more attention to cooking instead of clubbing, you would be able to make it by now.'

Suraya chuckled whilst dabbing pepper tears from her cheeks. 'You would think she had never been young,' she said to Monster, her tabby cat, when the conversation ended.

Grabbing her coat, Suraya jumped into the car and sped off down the road to the supermarket. It was a gloriously sunny, ice-cold winter's day - and busy, judging by the number of cars in the car park. Revving up the engine as she approached the speed bumps, she drove around once and in one manoeuvre parked the car in the Disabled bay.

'I'll only be a minute,' she shouted to the young blond boy in a red and white woollen bobble hat. Pushing a long line of trolleys, each one laced with silver tinsel, he pointed without speaking towards the rear of the car park, where the parking attendant was on duty. Suraya gave the boy the thumbs up and circled the car park for a second time, finally reversing into a tight spot between a Land Rover and a vintage Mini convertible with the top down.

Suraya had a weakness for vintage things - in fact, for anything old. She had trained as an antiques dealer, but when she struggled to find work she retrained and became a nurse. Peering nosily inside the Mini, she noticed an elderly man sitting in the driving seat. He wore a brown leather aviator hat with matching leather jacket lined with lamb's wool, and on his face he sported gold-rimmed sunglasses above a grey handlebar moustache.

'Uncle Govind, is that you?' she asked. Her astonished expression must have amused him because he burst out laughing.

'Are you OK?' she wanted to know, pointing to his hand, which was bound in a fresh white bandage. He pulled his sunglasses down to the tip of his nose.

'Pay no attention to this,' he said, raising his hand. 'It's just a little burn. The nurse at the walk-in clinic bandaged it up for me.' He joked, 'I should have waited until I got home to take a painkiller; now I'm seeing two of everything.'

He laughed again and his handlebar moustache spread across his small round face.

Govind, a retired car salesman, had sold everything from beaten-up Cortinas to second-hand Bentleys in his heyday; most of them from the street outside his house. He had a thirst for fast cars and horses - a throwback to his former life as a stable hand on a sugar estate in British Guiana. For a brief moment, he had become a famous jockey with a reputation that spread all the way along the Berbice River. It was the recession that had forced him into early retirement and now he spent his days reliving his past at the local betting shop.

'Wait there,' Suraya said, patting his shoulder through the window. 'I'll be back in a mo - you're coming home with me.'

'Jingle Bells' was blaring out of the loudspeakers when the supermarket door opened. Ducking her head, Suraya was given a garland of tinsel from a shop assistant dressed as Santa. She picked up a basket and headed off towards the aisles.

'Where are they?' she whispered impatiently, weaving in between the customers who hovered around the supermarket shelves. Cleaning stuff, loo rolls, washing-up liquid . . . she glided along past them in a tearing hurry.

Distracted by the thought of her uncle sitting in the cold car park in the open-topped Mini, she bumped into another shop assistant, this one dressed as Rudolf the Red-Nosed Reindeer. He pointed to aisle number seven.

Eggs, butter, spoons, candles, sugar . . . plates! She seized a couple and headed towards the checkout.

White lights guided Suraya across the car park. Her uncle had already closed the roof and locked up his Mini and was leaning against the bonnet of her car.

'I don't want to be any trouble,' he said, following Suraya around the car as she opened the passenger door.

'Uncle, you are no trouble,' she replied, putting the plates carefully on the back seat. 'Maya will love to see you.' She bit her lip as she fastened his seatbelt. Uncle Govind had a reputation for being provocative.

*

'Red or white?' Suraya said, holding up two bottles of wine.

Maya pointed to the bottle of red and whispered mischievously in Suraya's ear as the wine glugged in the glass. 'You're very brave. Mum's going to be mad when she finds out that you invited Uncle. You know how awkward he can be.' Maya was the cautious type. She was the oldest in the family - married, sensible and very predictable.

'What else could I do? Did you see his hand?' Suraya looked at Peter, who held out his glass.

'Shh, he's coming,' she added.

Uncle Govind came out of the bathroom, picking at the bandage on his hand. He popped two pills in his mouth and swallowed them as if a spoonful of cod liver oil had just slipped down his throat.

'I like the picture of the Kaieteur Falls in there,' he said, leaning on the back of Peter's chair.

'It's one of British Guiana's wonders. There isn't a waterfall in the world that can match that one. Did you know that it's named after an ancient Amerindian who threw himself over the falls to save his village?'

Suraya winked at Maya, picked up a plate and poured steaming dhal over the rice.

'Now, where shall I sit?' Uncle Govind asked.

'Anywhere you like, Uncle,' Suraya replied, waiting to hand him the plate.

He frowned. 'Anywhere is like telling me to sit nowhere,' he said. 'Do you think the Chief of the

Kaieteur Falls sat "anywhere"?' He stretched over Peter's plate for the pepper sauce.

'When he sat in his canoe,' the old man continued, 'he knew where he belonged. It was his right to be there and he knew who he was.' Uncle Govind puffed out his chest. 'And where will Shanti sit? I thought she was coming,' he said.

'She's late,' Suraya sighed. 'You can take her seat until she gets here.'

'So I have a temporary seat,' he said, sitting down next to Peter.

By now, Suraya was already beginning to regret her invitation but her anxieties soon faded as the evening wore on. Uncle Govind seemed to settle down, sharing his love of cars with Peter, who listened attentively. His shoulders were less hunched and she noticed that he had slipped off his shoes. Even Maya was captivated by his storytelling. Suraya kept the food and wine flowing until all the pots were empty. She watched Uncle Govind twiddle his moustache in satisfaction.

After dinner, Suraya collected the plates and took them to the kitchen, returning to the lounge with a tray of cheesecake and chocolates. She dimmed the lights and switched on the lamp so as to create a cosy, warm atmosphere. The smell of cinnamon drifted through the air from the scented candles she had lit in the fireplace.

'Let's have the dessert on the sofa,' she suggested. 'Uncle Govind, you come and sit here by me.'

The night was going smoothly. Suraya related the story of how she had met Uncle Govind at the supermarket. Maya told her uncle how she had got a promotion at work and how Peter had bought a new car, a Mercedes. Uncle Govind immediately dismissed the Mercedes, favouring a vintage MG.

Enjoying the lively conversation, Suraya brought out a family photo album and they all picked out old photographs that reminded them of special times during their lives.

'You were so handsome,' Suraya said to her uncle. She pointed to him posing by the coconut tree back home. He wore knee-length trousers and a cotton shirt with a single breast pocket over his left side.

'I take after your grandmother,' he said, winking, and he turned the page.

Suddenly he stopped, and brought the album closer to his face. He leaned towards the lamp for a better view, smoothing down the plastic covering on the page.

'Where did you get this picture?' he asked.

Suraya leaned over Uncle Govind's shoulder to take a closer look. Her mother had brought the album round one day and asked her to scan some photos from it, but she had never really taken much notice of it before.

'I haven't seen this photo in years,' he said.

He was staring at a group of young men posing in front of a painted background of coconut trees and a long winding stream. A table, with a plastic fern in a china pot on top, was placed in the middle of the picture as if to give it a 3D effect.

'I wonder where those boys are now,' he sighed nostalgically.

Suraya wished that she had a camera right at that moment, for his whole face had brightened up as if he was looking at a pot of gold.

'This one, he worked with me in the factory,' he said, pointing to a short man with a quiff.

'We used to call him Jet Black, because his hair was so dark and shiny. I think he used to rub coconut oil on it all the time. And this fella, see his movie star looks? He had all the girls after him, so his name was Sweet Boy.'

Uncle Govind ran his fingers along the photograph and called out the names of every one of his friends. And then his body sank a little in the chair.

'How your grandmother cried that day,' he reminisced, sighing deeply. 'This picture was the last one we took before we left for England. It was an exciting and sad day at the same time. Imagine, one minute you have your whole family around you and then . . .,' he slapped his hands together, '. . . bam! Your whole family is gone. I left, your mother left, Desree, Carmen, Carmel, Marvin. Imagine, our mother watched us all go, she didn't know if any one of us was alive or dead. We had no Facebook and all those things that you have now. If I missed your grandmother so much, just imagine how much she missed me. Now that is what you call sacrifice.'

Uncle Govind leaned his head back on the sofa and closed his eyes for a moment as if he was meditating. 'On my last night we sat around at your grandmother's house, telling old stories just like this. She sat right next to me, holding my hand.' He quickly lifted his head and reached for Suraya's hand. Holding it tight, he continued, 'We had just eaten a plate of food, dhal and rice and roti, no meat like tonight, just dhal and rice like in the old days. You couldn't get any more than that anyway. She told us how she used to go and fetch the rations for her mother with a rice sack. They had some salt, ghee, some salt fish, split peas and rice and sometimes a little piece of tamarind. That was all,' he said, massaging the tips of Suraya's fingers. 'How they suffered - and we made them suffer even more when we left.'

He licked his lips and his sadness faded. 'I need a drink,' he said. 'Do you have any rum in the house?'

Suraya did, but mindful that he was on medication, she shook her head.

'Guyanese girls with no rum? Whatever next! Peter, pass me my jacket.' He pulled a hip flask from the inside pocket. 'For medicinal purposes only,' he said, grinning, and took a double shot before turning the page. 'Suraya, do you have a magnifying glass?' he asked.

Suraya smiled cheekily at Maya before going off to rummage through a drawer in the hallway.

When she returned, she saw Uncle Govind take another swig from his hip flask. She handed him the magnifying glass and watched him scrutinise the picture, holding the glass close to his eye. He moved it around, distorting the faces in the black and white photograph.

'Look - here is your grandmother,' he said, pointing to a picture of a proud-looking woman. She was in a tropical garden with palm trees on either side of her. Wearing a scarf on her head, like a bandana, she leaned on a small picket fence and smiled proudly at the camera.

'That is the lady we left behind. How would you feel, Suraya, if your sister had to leave you behind?'

Suraya leaned over again and took a long hard look at the picture of her grandmother. Then she gave a shiver, as if someone had walked over her grave.

'I would want to die,' she said, looking over at Maya. 'I would want to hold her back and tell her not to leave.'

'That's exactly what our mother did do,' Uncle Govind said, and tears collected in his eyes. He went on: 'And you, Maya, what would you do, if Suraya or Shanti left you?'

The mention of Shanti's name reminded Suraya that her sister still hadn't arrived. She got up and sent her a text. *Hope you're ok. Let me know all is well.*

'Well, Maya?' her uncle said again. 'What would you do?'

'Uncle,' Maya said, taking his hand, 'I would give Suraya and Shanti my blessing and tell them that they could always call on me for help. Sometimes people have to leave us. That's a sacrifice too, to let people go. I'm sure Grandma would have wanted you to come and better your life, no matter how it hurt her. And you have made her proud.'

'So, do you regret leaving, Uncle?' Suraya asked gently. There were three candles on the coffee table and she lit them all. She watched Peter and Maya in the yellow glow waiting eagerly to hear the old man's reply.

Uncle Govind took a long time to answer the question. It seemed as if he was searching for the right words. They watched a tear roll down his face.

'What choice did I have?' he said, his voice faltering. 'If I wanted to live a better life, I had to leave. Her family did it long ago when they sailed on those terrible ships all the way from Madras. I travelled by sea to come here. I sat in a bunk at the bottom of the boat and sailed to a new world. The British wanted your ancestors to work on the plantations - and then they wanted us again.'

Uncle Govind took another shot of rum and closed his eyes. His bandaged hand slipped down and hung over the arm of the sofa. Suraya carefully prised his hip flask from his other hand. Then she took the duvet from her bed and laid it over him, tucking in the sides.

Suraya and her dinner-party guests quietly took the dishes from the coffee table and carried them into the kitchen. A few minutes later, she was waving them off from the upstairs window, her breath creating little clouds of steam on the glass as she followed the lights of the car down to the end of the road. There was a light dusting of snow on the ground.

Her phone bleeped as she pulled the curtains shut. It was a text from Shanti. *Sorry I didn't make it. I'm ok. Any dhal puri left? Speak tomorrow x.*

Suraya blew each one of the candles out and switched off the light in the lounge. She tucked her uncle's injured hand under the duvet. Picking up the photo album, she smoothed out the plastic covering that lay over her grandmother's photo and tiptoed towards the lit candle on the mantelpiece. Leaning towards the warm yellow flickering light, she whispered, 'Thank you for letting them go.'

The Natal Baby

Durban, 1887

NELU HAD GOOD reason to run away. She wanted to protect her unborn child. Three months ago, her friend Ramu's baby son was taken away from her, soon after he was born. The Planter said the child was sick, that the mother's lack of hygiene was the cause. He had refused to send for the doctor. The Planter said they did not have money to waste on people like her.

Ramu cried for weeks after the little body was removed. I heard that they buried him in the ground somewhere at the base of the rolling hill, three hours' walk from here. It was not the Hindu way - but what choice did she have when the Planter had forbidden us from cremating our babies?

It was Devki who told me that Nelu was planning to leave that same night. 'She's afraid the manager will send his men to take her baby, Radha,' she said, handing me a bundle of sugar cane. 'I'm really worried about her,' she added, brushing down her skirt that had become stained with the sticky yellow juice.

I looked over towards our hut, which lay past huge swathes of tall canes topped with emerald-green leaves waiting to be harvested. In the distance, down by the stream, I saw that the dusty old sugar sack which hung over the door as a curtain had been pulled aside. Had she already run away?

As I threw the bundle of cane into the cart, I stole another glance at the hut, and this time I saw her. Bird-like, with a swollen abdomen, she was limping along the grass verge that led down to the stream, clasping her belly as though concealing loaves of bread stolen from the kitchen in the big house at the top of the hill. When she disappeared behind the hut, I returned to Devki and knelt down beside her.

'We could help her disappear,' I murmured, watching the bare backs of the cane cutters as they slashed through the thick stalks like soldiers on the battlefield. They drove forward in rows; machetes raised high in the sky, chopping through the tough skin of the cane as they advanced further into the field.

'We will all die if we get caught,' she muttered, hunched over a stalk on the ground. She dragged it towards her, muttering angry words under her breath as it snagged on her shabby skirt. Devki's withered body was being pushed too hard. I helped her pull the cane up and clamp it under her arm.

'Would that be such a bad thing?' I said bitterly, scowling at the cane cutter Dhanraj, who had just thrown a long piece of cane in my direction, nearly hitting me - it landed mere inches away from my feet. I nudged Devki. He had heard us whispering in our own language.

I stared at him, at his black skin roasted by the heat; his turban - once white, now dirty grey - tied tightly around his head; his machete dangling down by his side.

Dhanraj and Nelu had arrived at the plantation together seven months ago. I can still see them now, sitting side by side on the wooden cart laden with supplies brought in from the Bluff. They were as hollow-eyed and starved as I had been when I arrived two months earlier.

Oh, that voyage from India to South Africa! There were times when I thought I was going to die, rolling about in the belly of the ship all day and night. Some men did not survive, and I prayed to my God that their souls would find peace when their bodies were unceremoniously thrown overboard. Without a funeral pyre, how could their lives begin again in the next world?

When we disembarked, we lined up in the dock, waiting to honour our contracts. 'Honour?' I snorted to myself now. 'The Planters don't know the meaning of the word here.' I was recruited to work here for five years doing 'light gardening' - that's what the man at the depot in Calcutta told me, but I never anticipated this hard, brutal life.

'Look at his back,' Devki tutted. 'The scars have still not healed.'

A few days after he arrived, Dhanraj stumbled and fell in the fields: for this simple accident, he received a terrible beating which nearly killed him. That had made him an angry, bitter man. But it was the salt that they poured on to his open wounds that changed him for ever. He did not cry out like the others, but sucked in his breath until his veins bulged out of his neck, his fists closing in until the palms of his hand bled. That is how they have remained ever since.

'Nelu's baby was nearly fatherless before it was born,' Devki continued, aware of his burning eyes on her. We heard the crack of a whip and he yanked at a stick of cane and chopped it down at its root. The blow was so strong, had he miscalculated, the blade would have severed his foot.

It jolted us too. We hurried to the cart and heaped more cane inside. Devki helped me tighten the sash around my waist. I covered my head with my scarf and hitched up my skirt, putting one foot on the wheel. Grabbing the bar that ran along the side of the cart, and with a push from Devki, I pulled myself up and jumped inside.

This used to be Nelu's job. The cane had to be sorted out in straight lines on the flat-bottomed wooden floor of the cart. We could pack more in this way. But then the baby began to feel like rocks in her womb and she couldn't carry on doing the work. The overseer said she could pick weeds from the young cane shoots instead. But we knew that that work would be scarce until the harvest was over. So now she sits alone in the hut all day waiting for the scraps of food that we share with her each night from our meagre rations. Sometimes we can hardly feed ourselves yet her belly grows hungrier every day.

From the top of the cart I could see the whole plantation. Lush green cane fields, as far as the eye could see. To the left, our hut with its low roof of dried leaves, tips blackened from the smoke of the fires we light at night. Closer by, and I saw the men, bare-chested, hacking away at the nut-brown stalks swollen with cane juice. A white line of oxen, their bones jutting through their leathery skins, waited along the dirt track to heave their loads up to the factory.

'*Of course!*' I exclaimed under my breath as the idea came to me.

I looked at their bony bodies again and followed the dirt track backwards around the bend to the right until it disappeared out of sight. Then I followed an imaginary line down the side of the cane field, ignoring the heavy chopping sound of metal and wood. There, almost hidden away from view by the sugar cane, was the disused stable. It was covered in vines and camouflaged in deep sea-green leaves. I jumped down from the cart flushed with excitement.

'The old stable where we used to mind the oxen - that's where she can stay,' I said to Devki. 'It's possible to reach it in half an hour if we keep to the edge of the field. In three days, the field will be cleared - that's more than enough time for Nelu to have her baby and rest a while after the birth.'

'It will be difficult for her to move that fast,' Devki commented, eyeing the overseer who kept tapping his leg menacingly with a long stick.

Devki was right. I had seen Nelu that morning, in the darkness before dawn, struggling to walk down to the stream, breathing heavily as she stepped over loose stones and rocks. At one point, she slipped and fell forwards, her hands plunging into the water. I tried to reach out to her, but she pushed me away and then sat back on her heels and stared up to the sky. It was filled with tiny shimmering stars that lit up her face in the darkness. She closed her eyes and I joined her in prayer.

*

That night, we shared less food with Nelu than normal. Before we ate I had scooped two spoonfuls of rice and some dhal from the cooking pot set on the fire just outside the hut and placed them in a wooden bowl. I ripped up an old sugar sack and, covering the bowl with it, I stashed it in a hole in the ground. I then rolled a large stone over the hole and went inside the hut.

Nelu and Devki were already lying on the floor near the door. As I lay beside Nelu, swirls of smoke drifted into the hut. I peeped outside through a gap in the wooden slats and saw Dhanraj, walking towards the fire, puffing on a long wooden pipe, his eyes fixed on the weakly flickering flames. A moth flew across his face and he batted it away, his fists still clenched. He tapped his pipe on a large rock, stooping down as he passed it, and headed for the door of our hut. Quickly, and making no sound at all, I lay back and pulled the blanket up to my chin.

He paused at the doorway, looking at the bodies sprawled around the floor. He saw Nelu's terrified eyes as he passed us - I am sure of it; how else can I explain the softening of his fists when he stepped over her?

A hush filled the hut, and when I was certain the others were sleeping, I turned to Devki, who had her back to me.

'Are you sure you want to come?' I whispered, remembering how she had struggled to pick up stalks earlier that day.

Silence was the only reply.

*

I must have dozed off when I felt Nelu's fingers creep like a spider over my hand and squeeze it tight. It was the signal I had been waiting for, ever since the last embers from the fire had died out and plunged us into darkness.

I looked around me and saw the others lying head to toe like fish in the market.

'Are you ready?' I whispered to Nelu, pulling my scarf over my head as we crept out of the hut. Clouds drifted across the moon as we tiptoed down to the water's edge. Devki was there, already waiting for us.

She handed me the parcel of food I had hidden away earlier. Then, tearing a strip of cloth from her skirt as I had done from mine, she dipped it into the water. As she did so, a small fish curled its tail and changed direction. She held the damp cloth to Nelu's round face.

'Keep this,' Devki murmured, catching her tears.

Nelu smiled warmly and kissed her cheek. 'We three are sisters now,' she said, turning and stretching out her hand to me.

But our peace was short-lived. As Nelu turned, she saw Dhanraj, standing at the top of the verge behind us. I could not tell how long he had been standing there nor how much he had heard, but as he took a step down towards us, we cowered like frightened children. I could see that he knew everything.

I stood in front of Nelu, shielding her from his fist as he brought it down. But it was not meant for her, and as I landed on the ground, the skin on my face stung from his blow. Nelu sank to her knees.

'Do not stop us,' she cried, pleading with him.

I watched helplessly as she curled her arms around herself to protect their baby. Dhanraj paused and brought his fists up to his face. Nelu touched him gently on his back, and for a brief moment, her head rested on his shoulder. Devki and I sat motionless, wondering what we should do. Dhanraj then did a remarkable thing. Devki saw it too: his gentle embrace, his tears, his hand on Nelu's belly.

As we gazed, he opened his right hand and took from it a small circle of string. It was as black as his hair and as tiny as a baby's wrist. It was the Indian way of warding off evil spirits. He handed it to her and then, cradling her in his arms, he helped her slowly and tenderly up to the top of the verge.

We followed them, clutching at damp clumps of earth on our way up. Devki stopped suddenly, her face so close to the ground she could have kissed the earth. Breathing heavily, she motioned me to carry on.

'I will slow you down,' she said, wiping away tears when she reached the top of the verge. 'But I will wait for your return.'

Without turning back, we covered our heads and disappeared into the darkness.

*

The next day, two more cane cutters arrived at the plantation. I had heard that the manager was keen to finish harvesting the field. They jumped off the cart by the factory wall and walked down the hill towards us, their machetes swinging from their hands. Devki had spotted them too, observing their silent, weary march in the white heat of the day. She turned and looked at me as the men passed the cart and went on to join the other men, slashing through stalks still rooted in the earth.

In the distance, I could just make out Dhanraj, throwing stalks on the ground. I had jumped down from the cart and was trying to tease a splinter from my hand when I heard the most terrifying howl.

The overseer ran across the field towards the men, who had formed a semicircle in the middle of a row of cane yet to be cut down. They were so close to the old stable I feared they had found Nelu inside. Devki heard it too and stepped forward, grabbing my hand. She began to run; her hair tied at the back of her head broke loose and streaked across her face. She tripped and nearly fell, her old bones giving way.

The men were standing side by side, shoulders touching, blocking our view. They spoke in their own tongue, hurriedly, urgently. The leaves of the sugar cane seemed to whisper as the men parted the matted cane stalks and held them back. That is when I left Devki, lying like a pile of old clothes on the ground, and sprinted towards the scene, gasping for breath.

The men held the stalks back as far as they could, while Dhanraj reached into the dark shadows and pulled out a small bundle. I slowed down, almost relieved. *It's not Nelu, it's not Nelu,* I repeated over and over in my head. Then horror struck me. I covered my face with my hands and screamed. There, dead, wrapped up in the sack, was a baby, not more than a few hours old. Thick black hair, dark skin, round face like his mother's . . . eyes shut. As if he were asleep.

The sky, the cane, the stream, the men . . . all disappeared from my sight. I saw only Dhanraj, his son in his arms.

Suddenly, someone grabbed me. I jolted and spun around and around, and as I fell to the ground in a dead faint, I glimpsed it, if only for a second - the tiny circle of string around his perfect wrist.

*

I never saw Nelu again. I heard that she was spotted scavenging at the bottom of the rolling hill, three hours' walk from here, trying to find her firstborn's grave. I hope it's not true. I'd like to think she managed to run away and is somewhere else now, somewhere happy, and is picking up stalks as she used to do.

REPORT OF THE INDIAN IMMIGRANTS
COMMISSION 1885-7
UMZINTO – THIRTY-FOURTH DAY

EXAMINATION OF DR. W.P. TRITTON
By Brigade-Surgeon Lewer

The Umzimkulu district was originally attached to my circle; it is one hundred and twelve miles from Umzinto, there and back.

I am satisfied with the supply of medicines and instruments in the Central Hospital.

I do not think that deaths occur on estates, without being reported to me. All cases, which I have attended up to death and, therefore, I have been able to certify as to the cause of death. As to the death of Chaddie's child on Mr. Hawksworth's estate on 13th March 1884, on receiving information of the death of that child, I wrote to Mr. Hawksworth asking him to enquire into the case and to see if there was any suspicion of foul play or if the death had been natural; I have his permission to bury the body in the latter case, and asked him to let me know in the former case, so that I might hold a post-mortem, if necessary: I did not think that it was necessary to inspect the body.

Mr. C. Reynolds told me, two or three days ago, that a coolie woman disappeared for three days in the cane and gave birth to a child there, and that, on returning to the estate, she did not report the matter, but stayed in her house, saying that she was ill. Some few weeks afterwards, when the cane was being cut, the body of an Indian child was found wrapped in clothes, in a deep composed state. This took place, I think, before I assumed office. If the manager had reported this illness to the Medical Officer then in charge of the estate, that officer would have discovered that the woman had recently given birth to a child, and enquiries would have been instituted. I heard that the woman afterwards ran away.

British Library IOR/1/pj/6/284, File 1476

Runaway

AS SOON AS Sunita boarded the plane she headed straight for the lavatory. Locking the door behind her, she tore her picture out of the newspaper and ripped it into tiny pieces. If she had a match she would have burnt them, right there in the sink. Instead, she lifted the toilet seat, sprinkled the scraps of paper like confetti down the chute and flushed them away.

Leaning against the door, she closed her eyes and took a moment to breathe. She was almost there. Turning on the tap, she washed her hands and looked closely at her reflection in the mirror. Her face looked older, harder. There were deep stress lines on her forehead and dark circles under her eyes. After brushing her hair, she pinched her cheeks until they glowed crimson red and pulled back the lock on the door.

The plane was filling up with passengers. They hustled past her trying to find their seats before it took off. Paul, her fiancé, sat in the aisle seat three rows in front of her next to a teenager with a golden tan who flexed his muscles to a group of girls on the other side of the plane. Quickly, Sunita walked along the aisle, thankful for the dim lights on board.

An excitable sun-burnt man covered in a mass of sea-green sequins and black feathers blew a whistle in Sunita's ear as she tried to return to her seat. Dancing in the aisle, he pulled her towards him. Flicking her hand at him as if she had just swatted a fly, she continued to push through the long line of passengers.

'I'm just having a laugh, love, no need to be so uptight,' he said, in a thick London accent. He dropped his hands to his sides to allow her to pass.

There was nothing that this tourist could teach her about the Trinidad Carnival. It was part of her DNA. When she was a child she had grown up watching her African friends dance in colourful costumes through the streets of Port of Spain. In the bright sunshine, she would stand on the edge of the pavement with her father behind her, his hands fixed firmly on her shoulders, and wiggle along to the exciting sounds of the steel drums as they passed by. Sometimes, she would tug at his hands, urging him to take her into the crowds to join her friends as they celebrated their African heritage, but he held her back.

It was at Indian weddings where Sunita celebrated her culture, following in her father's footsteps as a Tassa player. Throughout the night, they used to play to hundreds of people, beating the drums that hung around their necks with long sticks of dried-out sugar cane. Nizam, their Muslim neighbour in the village, taught her father how to become a champion Tassa drummer. Sunita, grateful for the distraction from her homework, would sit out on the verandah watching their bodies tighten as they thrashed at the drums. And when the neighbours complained about the noise, the two men played louder and faster, falling into their chairs laughing when they ended with the loudest beat of all.

Perhaps that was where Sunita got her rebellious streak from. She remembered that her dad had had such a carefree spirit then. He even joined in the carnival when it became more popular. Sunita joined in too, playing Tassa in a costume band to celebrate East Indian culture. It made her father proud to know that she was carrying on one of the great traditions of his Indian ancestors. Even though girls playing the drums was frowned upon in the community, he supported her. She wished he had continued to support her now. Despite her anger and his violent words in the weeks before she left, she believed he still loved her.

When she finally got to her seat, Sunita slumped down, out of breath as though she had crossed the finishing line in a marathon race. Dimming the overhead light, she placed the cushion on the floor, kicking it under the seat in front of her. She even dared to smile.

Just then, she spotted a middle-aged, fair-skinned Indian man heading towards her. He wore a dark suit, white shirt and black shoes, with a pair of stylish metallic sunglasses resting on the tip of his bony nose. He stood out in the crowd of tourists, looking like some kind of insurance agent. Having checked the seat number above Sunita's head, he looked at her through his dark lenses.

'May I sit?' he enquired, in a voice as smooth as molasses when Sunita did not react.

'Of course,' she replied, getting up and moving out into the aisle to let him pass. He stepped over her handbag like a stick insect.

As the air hostess pulled the heavy doors closed, Sunita looked up the aisle at Paul, who had craned his neck around to snatch a glance at her. She gave him the thumbs up. There was no turning back now.

'It's exciting, isn't it?' the man said, looking up at Sunita as she slid down the back of her chair on to the seat.

'What do you mean?' she asked, confused by his remark.

'To get away - away from everything,' he said, looking at her straight in the eyes. Sunita decided it was best not to engage in conversation. She took the in-flight magazine from the pocket in front of her and flicked through the pages.

'I'm Simon,' the man introduced himself. 'My friends call me Si. And you?' He picked up the cushion and placed it on her lap.

Sunita hesitated as she searched for words. 'Annie,' she replied eventually, turning her head as if someone had called her from the other side of the plane. The cool air fanned her face, burning under her make-up like hot coal.

'Hmm . . .,' said Si. 'I've met *a lot* of Annies in my time.'

The man's comment made Sunita feel nervous, watched, judged. She looked differently at him now. Perhaps he wasn't an insurance agent after all. He peeled back a sweet wrapper, revealing a ruby-red droplet the size of a tamarind seed.

'Sweet?' He proffered a white paper bag. 'It helps with the pressure,' he said, winking at her and grinning so widely she could see all of his teeth.

Sunita refused politely. She wanted to go down to see Paul but knew that she should wait, at least until after the plane took off. Her father had friends in high places, including at the airport. She caught her fiancé's eye and fluttered her lashes at him instead.

Paul always said that she had cat's eyes: beautiful, big brown eyes that slanted up at the edges like the curve of her lips when she smiled. She wondered if he would still feel the same in a year or two. Rajni, her best friend, doubted it. Her marriage had ended just a few weeks after her husband had placed the mangalsutra around her neck; she had balked at the gold necklace that was supposed to bring her good luck. Now, she had little positive to say about the union between man and woman - arranged or otherwise.

It was Rajni's defeatist attitude that had spurred Sunita on to leave that night. Rajni was the only person she could turn to.

'Just because our mothers put up with difficult men doesn't mean we have to,' Sunita said as they lifted her suitcase into the boot of Paul's car. 'I personally can't live like this any more,' she said, touching Rajni's fingers lightly as she climbed into the front passenger seat.

'You'd better look after her,' Rajni said, giving a meaningful look at Paul in the driving seat.

*

The white noise of the engines scrambled the voices in Sunita's head and then hummed quietly as the plane flew through the blackness towards London. A glint of gold caught her eye as Si yawned and pulled up the blanket that rested on his lap. His eyes fluttered for a moment and then closed. Sunita was grateful for his silence.

If only the locals in her village could have been as accommodating. She had taken a job as a salesgirl in her father's store. It was a stop-gap after her graduation. Her father was not shy in telling every customer that Sunita was going to teach their sons and daughters. He was proud; his only daughter, a Brahmin, had returned home to teach his people. It was something to be celebrated.

Soon, children in bows and braces followed their mothers into the store bearing gifts for their future teacher. Within weeks, Sunita had acquired a box of scented soaps, nail polish and hand creams. She had become something of a local celebrity and was enjoying the attention, until Paul, bold as brass, had walked into the store one hot afternoon and set an apple on the counter.

Although she would never admit it to him now, he was the most good-looking man she had ever seen.

*

'Would you like coffee or tea?' the stewardess asked, interrupting Sunita's thoughts as she parked the drinks trolley next to her.

As Sunita ordered coffee, she sneaked a quick glance over at Paul. He was reaching for the light above his head. He loved reading. As a graduate in law, he had dreams of setting up his own firm in Port of Spain. Books, newspapers, manuals, the small writing on the back of milk cartons - he scrutinised them all. On the first day she had agreed to meet him, at the old railway station, he was clutching a newspaper in one hand and a hardback book in the other, the title obscured by his long fingers.

They sat chatting on a splintered bench set in a black cast-iron frame a stone's throw from the disused track. Sometimes they sat in silence or held hands in the shadows of the corrugated iron roof that hung over its crumbling walls. As the months passed, they grew bolder.

Sunita sipped her coffee. She wanted to be with him, to tell the teenager with the big muscles to swap with her - but she didn't dare. It was unlikely that any of these tourists would read the local papers, but when her father put the 'Missing' ad in the personal columns, she couldn't risk being seen with him. The air hostess was busy rifling through cans of Coke, lemonade, bitter lemon, still water, fizzy water and tonic water on the trolley, searching for tomato juice.

Si peered into Sunita's cup. 'You should have a Bloody Mary,' he said, nudging her. 'The vodka will calm your nerves.' He then held his hand up to receive the bloody red glass that passed over Sunita's head.

Blood had been spilt on the day that she and Paul had decided to elope. The couple had been seen linking arms on the university campus just outside Port of Spain. It was only for a moment. He had been walking backwards, pointing to the room where he lived as a student, when he stumbled. Sunita had caught him, that was all - but it was their interlocking arms that her uncle had seen. Five seconds was all it took for Sunita's life to change.

That evening, she returned home to find the house plunged in darkness. The air was filled with the familiar sound of tree frogs whistling as she approached the unlocked door. A tiny gecko scrambled up the wall as she tiptoed along the hallway. She listened for her mother's shrill voice singing her favourite Indian songs on the radio, or the sudden clap of fresh roti as she cooked in the kitchen. There was nothing, however, except for a trail of light leading to the kitchen at the back of the house.

'Where have you been?' her father asked solemnly, his fingers wrapped around the neck of a half-empty bottle of rum. Splinters of crystal cut glass scratched and cracked under the soles of her shoes as she walked towards the kitchen table.

He did not wait for an explanation. Staggering to his feet, he let the chair fall backwards, bouncing on the tiled floor. He kicked it to one side as he ran his hands along the kitchen worktop towards a picture of his mother on the wall. A garland of beads, red and white, hung from its frame.

'Ma,' he pleaded with his hands clasped as though in prayer. 'Is this what you came here for? Struggled all those years for?'

Sunita's mouth dried up. She steadied her shaking hands on the table where a pocket knife lay at its centre.

'You are an Indian! Since when do you think you can hang about with that African boy?' her father bellowed indignantly. Lurching over to the table, he banged it so loudly that the dishes piled on the draining board crashed to the floor.

He picked up his pocket knife and opened it. Running the blade slowly and deliberately across his palm, he caused tiny trickles of blood to ooze out, filling the criss-cross lines mapped out on his hand.

'These hands bled on the cane fields so that you could have a better life,' he shouted, throwing the knife down on the table. 'Get out, get out!' he screamed.

Sunita ran up the stairs to her room and fell to her knees. Shame riddled her body. Her father was right - she had betrayed him. She knew that to choose Paul, a black man, over her own would break her father's heart, but she did it anyway. Two generations, born and bred on the island, was not enough to erase the hatred that had been nurtured all those years ago. One race pitched against the other by the British for their own gain. But Trinidad was not India.

And then she sat up and pulled her suitcase out from its place underneath the bed.

'Times have changed,' she mumbled, checking the door behind her. 'And you can't go back to the way things were.'

Soon after that, her picture had appeared in the paper under the headline: *Missing*. The search was on to find Sunita, but Sunita was long gone.

*

The shutter slammed as Si tugged it down to block out the night sky. It jolted Sunita. He then bumped her arm as he pulled the tray table down in front of him, and, when she flinched, he held his hand up to hers and bowed his head in a gesture of gracious apology.

'Don't you ever take your sunglasses off?' she asked him curiously, pressing the button on the side of her armrest until their chairs were even.

'Nope, not when I'm working,' he said. He brushed flecks of dust off the table with the back of his hand.

'Here, I have a tissue in my bag,' she said, rummaging through the contents of her handbag. Her fingers settled on her purse, thick and fat with layers of dollars that Rajni had thrust into her hand when they departed. She would have to find a job quickly; Paul's best friend from university would not be able to put them up for long in his flat in West London. Sunita had met Derrick only a few times. He was a nice enough man but she wasn't sure how much he approved of her relationship with Paul. Whenever she spoke to Derrick, he always avoided looking her in the eye, but preoccupied himself with other things, like resetting the time on his watch or playing with the food on his plate. Perhaps he thought Paul was giving up too much to be with her.

'Thank you,' Si said, bowing his head again, spreading the tissue out on the tray table. His cheeks rolled forward as he looked down, concentrating on the folds he had created - two in all. Then he slid it to the corner of the table, placing his empty glass on top like a paperweight.

He leaned into her as he pulled his wallet out of his trouser pocket and set two passport photos one by one, face down, on the table. They lined up like tarot cards.

Sunita sat up, watching closely as Si, like a magician, extended his arms so that she could see the cufflinks on his shirt. For a moment, she was enjoying the drama of it all. She peered over the tops of the seats in front of her to see Paul's reading light still shining, then drew her face closer to Si's so she could get a clear view of the pictures on either side. He flipped the first photo over and looked for a reaction.

Her smile lingered in a momentary paralysis as she saw Paul's face appear on the upturned card.

'I don't understand,' she said, retreating.

Si cracked his knuckles and moved swiftly on to the second one, his thumb flicking at its edge.

Sunita tried to focus. Her hands pressed against her throbbing temples.

'Me?' she cried out. It was the same photograph that had appeared in the papers. 'Who the hell *are* you?'

He picked the photo up, held it high above his head, and twisted it round. He then lifted his sunglasses for the first time, looked at her and spoke.

'Your father wants you back.'

Sugar Is Our Thing

I COULD HAVE slapped the manager, Mrs Dean, after she accused me of lying. But, of course, I didn't – what would be the point of that? I would lose a job that I could not afford to lose, while she would get all the sympathy.

There were three of us who had gone for the supervisor's job. Edith and Samantha sat closest to Mrs Dean's office on a short row of wooden chairs lined up against the wall. Their mouths dropped open when they saw me. To be honest I was just as surprised as they were when I was asked to go for an interview, but if there was a chance for a little bit more money and a break from endlessly watching 2lb bags of sugar shunt past me on the conveyor belt, I was going to take it. The chair furthest away from Mrs Dean's door was empty so I sat there, put my hands on my lap and studied a ladder in my tights.

Mrs Dean had her fingers dipped in a tall filing cabinet by the window when I was eventually called in. I sat down in front of her desk while she leafed through the papers. After a while, she pulled out my file, banged the drawer shut with her hip and sank into her seat opposite me. She was looking angry.

I braced myself and started to flex my fingers under the table the moment she opened her mouth - and I'm not a violent person. I have seen too much of that kind of thing. Anyway, if I kicked up a fuss, Mrs Dean would probably call the police on me. I'd be arrested, convicted and sentenced all in the same day.

Did I like working at the factory? How did I get along with the other ladies? She wanted to know. I breathed a sigh of relief, as it seemed that the interview was going all right after all. This was until she started asking me all sorts of other questions that had nothing to do with the job. Where did I come from? What did 'Indo-Caribbean' mean? Where was Guyana? Then she started arguing with me. 'You're not from the West Indies, are you? You look more Indian than West Indian to me!'

Things had turned nasty. She started to shout at me, as though I couldn't understand English.

'WHY DON'T YOU JUST TELL THE TRUTH AND BE DONE WITH IT?' she bellowed across the desk, pushing up her thick black glasses that always slipped down her face when she sucked in her cheeks before shouting at someone.

'WHY SHOULD I?' I shouted back at her in my head. 'IT'S NONE OF YOUR DAMN BUSINESS!'

That was when I stopped listening to her and thought of the slap that I itched to give her. I flinched as I imagined the commotion that would ensue. I pictured her smug face watching me from the window, while I pushed my way through the factory turnstile gates, never to return, with my belongings hurriedly stuffed in my handbag. Mrs Dean had always thought I was a troublemaker who needed to be taught a lesson – at least, that's what she said when I refused to stay past my shift last week. I suddenly realised that she had absolutely no intention of giving me the supervisor's job. This was just her way of putting me in my place. I ground my teeth and kept my cool.

No way would I give her the satisfaction of sacking me. I would rather walk out of the job myself. I knew I could always go back to sewing fancy dress costumes at home. My old boss, Raymond, would have me back in a heartbeat.

Raymond was so fat that when he pushed his way inside the boarding house where we both lodged, his bulk would make the front door bang against the wall, tearing up the floral wallpaper and causing bits of plaster to fall on the floor. It made our widowed landlady, Dorothy Maps, come out a few times. Mrs Maps didn't bother to speak to me, she just frowned and gestured at the mess as if it was my job to get the dustpan and brush out and sweep it up. She's all right though - there aren't many around here who would rent out a couple of rooms to Indian people like us.

Raymond tried to keep on her good side too. Once he gave her a long feather boa like the singers wear on stage. It was as if she'd been showered in gold, she was so happy - and I was happy too. As long as I stitched together twenty-five cowboy suits a day, Raymond treated me with respect. The more work I did, the more work I got - and the more money I made. It was that simple.

Trouble was, after a while I got bored and lonely. It was nice to get out of the house now and again instead of being cooped up all day long just listening to the constant dull drumming of the sewing machine. By the evening my fingers looked like I had been in a cockfight - torn to strips, they were, and red raw from pulling and cutting cotton. That was when I asked my best friend Didi if there were any vacancies at the factory where she worked.

I met Mrs Dean on the first day I started on the factory floor packing sugar into bags. I sensed immediately that she didn't like me. She was a clean-looking woman with bright blue eyes as clear as glass marbles that followed me as she crossed the factory floor. Back and forth, back and forth she went, with her hands behind her back, watching me lift the sides of the paper bags so the sugar would fall straight in from the chute over my head. She was just like those overseers on the sugar estate in Guyana, always pushing us to do double the work for half the pay.

What I don't understand is why Mrs Dean had to be so rude. Imagine accusing me of lying like that – as if I don't know where I come from! Just because we're brown doesn't mean we are all the same. My husband Dan looks Indian, so do Didi, Ramesh, Krishna and Lakshmi - but they're not from India. Ha! My name is Rose, and no one asks *me* if I'm English. Sometimes, even I get confused. There's this lady who runs a shop on the corner where we live - Varsha, her name is. She's from Mauritius. What would Mrs Dean make of her, I ask myself. Technically, she's African!

I can still feel that woman getting under my skin even though I was sent to her office two hours ago. It's that rumbling voice of hers - like a sack of potatoes tumbling down the stairs.

While I'm brooding like this, Dan keeps glancing at me, even though most of the time he takes no notice of me at work. He's always checking that temperature gauge as if the place will blow up if he looks away for a second. I know he's anxious. If I got the promotion we'd be able to move house, the two of us. With the extra money, we could afford to take on a mortgage and repay Arnold Singh the loan for the deposit. We'd have a place to eat where the crumbs wouldn't fall in our bed - and what I wouldn't do for a bathroom of my own!

We could move right away from here. I've been thinking about North London. Didi says it's really posh out that way. Here in East London it is OK too; there are a couple of nice fellows from Guyana who run a stall in the market on Petticoat Lane, selling leather coats. I wonder how they got into a business like that? The rag trade is usually what the Bangladeshis do, not us.

Sugar is more our thing. I offered to get one of them a job at the factory once. There were loads of vacancies then. It seemed natural, somehow, to work there. What we didn't know about sugar was not worth knowing. Surprisingly, they turned me down flat. Didn't want to pick up where they left off, they said.

I don't think I could tell Dan if I didn't get the promotion. It would spoil his dinner. When he's upset, his bottom lip sort of droops down like it's going to curl over his chin and hug his Adam's apple.

Perhaps I should have told him what happened straight away instead of popping into the Ladies after my interview. That way, Eileen wouldn't have got to him first. Eileen, with her pencilled-on eyebrows and powdered nose; she's always ready to talk to my husband. She's got that meddling look in her eye, like a soup when it needs a stir and all the vegetables are stuck at the bottom. If she comes over here, maybe I'll slap *her*! Hugging him like that in front of everyone . . . I think she fancies him. If I can't slap Mrs Dean, then Eileen will do nicely.

'What's she saying to him, Didi? Can you hear them?' When I whisper to Didi she always jumps as if a jumbi's just tapped her on the shoulder. According to her, the spirits followed us all the way here from the plantation at Port Mourant.

Didi is one of my best friends. I love her as if she was my own sister. We've looked out for each other since we were children. I don't know how she's managed to keep her figure so well. I guess that's what happens when you don't have any children. Back home, all the boys wanted to marry her. They'd come to her house after church on Sundays and hang around the yard. But she was never interested. Her mum and dad used to go crazy! 'Trade her in for a couple of cows and a goat,' I would cheekily advise them, but I didn't really mean it. Instead, I wished I'd had her strength to say no.

Now look at her. She's got time for herself; time to check her face in the mirror in the morning to make sure her lipstick, red like a cherry, hasn't stuck to her teeth, and to plump up her hair and check for ladders in her tights. Oh, I could go on and on! If I get the promotion, she'll come and lodge with us in North London. I don't think I could live without her now.

Thinking about it, I *was* a troublemaker back home too, and Didi was always covering up for me. Like the time that I rode Doubles, the manager's mule, on the sugar estate. And we used to call all the boys names. Devendra was a skinny little boy we nicknamed Half-

Bake because his skin was so light. Ha! All the boys had nicknames in those days, such as Long Neck, Double Chin, Smallie, Shortie, Fish Mouth. We could be so cruel sometimes.

So, Half-Bake was coaxing the mule to walk along the side of the canal. The stupid animal was tied to the punts that looked like shallow rowing boats full with sugar cane. Me and Didi were walking to school one morning and when I saw Half-Bake dragging that mule along, I ran right up to him and asked if I could have a ride. He shook his head like a baby's rattle at first but soon changed his mind when I told him that I'd push him in the trench where the alligator would eat him. Ha! What a morning that was. I felt like Her Majesty the Queen.

Anyone would think that Mrs Dean was the Queen, the way she carries on. Didi says she wants to see me again. And now Dan is looking at me, and his bottom lip is beginning to swell. If she sacks me, I'll think to myself, so what? Sometimes these people need to learn that they can't push us around any more.

Patting down my apron to look tidy isn't going to make this any easier. I had better hurry up. I can hear those potatoes starting to tumble down the stairs. I'm worried - who wouldn't be? I've got a lot to lose. My daughter Angeli is waiting for me back home. If I could get the promotion, I'd be able to bring her over to London.

I'll never forget the terrible scene she made at the port when I left her. She screamed as if a snake had bitten her when I got on board the boat. A mother shouldn't be without her child. And Angeli is too young to be left on her own. It's true she's with her grandma and grandpa. Tata loves her like a psalm in his prayer book. He used to comb her long black hair as straight as an arrow, pushing at her shoulder to keep still as he brushed out the knots. He was good at it too.

'It's like brushing the tail of a donkey,' he would say when he'd finished. No wonder, after all those years spent mucking out the stables and hanging around horses. But love is love - and he loved those horses and he loved his granddaughter.

Love? We're a bit short of that around here - and now I'm starting to feel all hot and bothered. I have to find a way to keep my cool. I can't let Mrs Dean get the better of me. Maybe she's right - we *are* all Indians, just a different sort - and if she doesn't care what sort, then why should I? What makes an Indian anyway? It's just a piece of paper that she wanted me to tick, so why don't I just let her tick it. I'm brown, that's all she needs to know. It doesn't matter if I eat roti or chapatti; wear a sari or a pencil skirt; if you're brown, you're brown.

I'm not hearing anything any more, only the faint ring of the bell. It's like I'm stuck in the bath with my head under the water. I can hear my heartbeat, though. It's steady and fast. I can see Dan pushing back his cap, watching me climb up the stairs to the office. Didi's got her hand over her mouth as if she's holding in a breath, and Eileen . . . Eileen's got her hands on her hips. She's standing much too close to Dan. I wonder what she'd say if I said she could have him? Ha! What would she do then? Some of these girls want a bit of brown sugar in their tea to liven things up a bit.

The foreman is shuffling our team out of the factory. There'll be a new shift starting soon. He's got his arm around Dan, and is practically pushing him out of the door. Dan doesn't want to leave without me, I can tell. I can't go any faster though, my legs are feeling so heavy. And there is Mrs Dean, leaning on the railing at the top of the stairs, waiting for me. Her arms are folded and she's drumming her fingers on her jacket sleeve. Those bright blue eyes are fixed on mine and I am clenching my fists again.

*

The more work I do, the more work I get and the more money I make - that's what I tell Raymond when he walks in with his bulging black sacks. Ha! I'm making Red Indian outfits now. I notice that he's lost a bit of weight, although the door still bangs when he comes in.

Mrs Maps is sitting with me, picking off little stray strands of cotton from a headdress. It's nice to have her as company. She's a fast learner, wrapping the cotton around her finger and pulling it hard so that it snaps. Sometimes she bites it with her teeth. She doesn't need the money - I think she's here just to catch another glimpse of Raymond.

I saw Didi yesterday. I like it when she pops in on her way home. She said that Mrs Dean's still doing the rounds, staring hard at all the brown people. Thinking back on it, she was never going to give me a promotion. People like her don't do things like that for people like me. She was just fooling with me. Oh yes, and Didi said that Eileen's got a real sour face on her these days, as if she's sucking on a lemon, now that Dan's left. Didi's cousin Harry got in touch when he heard Dan was out of work, and my husband's training to be a welder now in Willesden. Soon, I'll pay off what I owe on the sewing machine and we'll have a bit more cash. Heaven knows, we need it.

I saw the boys from Petticoat Lane Market the other day. They were busy packing up their stall but had time enough to tell me that there were some jobs going at the biscuit factory in Wood Green. I'll ask them again when I see them on Sunday. We might even get to move to North London after all - Didi included.

FEATURE – CHUTNEY VILLAGE SOUVENIR
EDITION 2000
REPRODUCED WITH THE KIND PERMISSION
OF SURESH RAMBARAN
Indo-Caribbeans in the UK by Jim Jhinkoo, The Editor

To illustrate our position in this country I shall try to relate a short story. In 1970 I started work in the finance department of a local authority and was probably the only Indo-Caribbean person amongst over three thousand employees. Five years later, I filled in an application form for another position and entered 'Indo-Caribbean' as my race. I was summoned to Personnel and confronted by two female officers, one white and the other black. They told me I could not put 'Indo-Caribbean' on the form because there is no such thing, and in any case, they did not have that category in their Equal Opportunities monitoring programme. I was told I should change it to Indian, Pakistani or even Afro-Caribbean since I was from the West Indies. At that stage a senior personnel officer entered the room and after some discussions about race and migration she agreed that there were 'Indians' in the Caribbean because she had heard about Sonny Ramadhin, believed Rohan Kanhai was one of the best batsmen she had seen and thought Alvin Kallicharan was a cute little thing. The conclusion was that I could list myself as Indo-Caribbean – thanks to cricket.

Identity

London, 2010

'COME AGAIN?' INDIRA said when she first heard the solicitor speak. 'You are joking! Here's my passport and driving licence, Council Tax statement and electricity bill. You asked for two forms of identity and I've brought you four. So, what is the problem?'

She flicked back her curls and fidgeted with her skirt, waiting for the solicitor's reply.

Taking his time, he folded his arms and rested them on his desk, which was crowded with framed photographs of his wife, children and grandchildren. Then, tapping the corner of her aunt's will, he peered over the pictures and altered the lamp so that he could see Indira's face more clearly.

'The problem is, Ms Ramkeesoon,' he began sheepishly, 'I cannot confirm who you actually are.' He coughed when he saw the alarm on Indira's face.

'First of all, you call yourself Indira,' he went on, looking at the papers in front of him. 'But your first name is actually Clarence. Then there is the spelling of your surname. When I match it against your aunt's

- I mean my client's - they are totally different. It is not that I don't believe you - I am sure that you are who you say you are - but your surname is Ramkeesoon, and your aunt's,' he corrected himself again, 'I mean my client's, is Ramkishore. You can see the difficulty.'

Patience had never been one of Indira's virtues, especially when it came to people in authority. Her face darkened as the solicitor picked up the papers and shuffled them so that they all lined up in a neat pile, then bound them in a folder marked *Ramkishore*. He tied it up with a piece of red string, never once taking his eyes off Indira.

Determined to have her say, she dug deep to find her most sarcastic voice.

'Mr Whateveryoucallyourself. What exactly do you think has happened here? Was I switched at birth, left under a bush by a stork?'

The solicitor stared at Indira and there was a shocked silence. Suddenly, she jumped up out of the soft black leather chair, picked up her letters and bills and stuffed them back in her handbag.

'I am who I say I am,' she declared fiercely, pointing to her chest as if to confirm her own existence. 'As God is my witness,' she added, quoting one of her late aunt's favourite sayings, 'I am telling the truth.' Then she marched out, slamming the door behind her.

In the outer office, a pink-faced and permed middle-aged woman sitting behind her desk swivelled around in her chair to face Indira. She had heard every angry word.

'Young woman, you should be ashamed of yourself,' she snapped. 'Respect the dead as though they were still alive. If you are who you say you are, then you do not need God to prove it. Just go to the council and pick up the necessary papers. It's as simple as that!'

It was good advice, clean and straightforward like a thick black line drawn with a ruler down a crisp white sheet of paper. If only Indira's story was that straightforward.

Standing outside the solicitor's office on Tottenham Court Road, Indira looked up and down at the endless stream of anonymous faces of people who jostled past her. Crowds spilled out onto the street from shops and coffee bars. A little girl clutching a teddy the colour of candyfloss ran over Indira's feet. Little mitten-hands pulled her mother along in the direction of a shop with flashing bright lights and stacks of toys. As they snaked past Indira, the little girl's mother grabbed her husband's arm and dragged him along. There, right in front of Indira's eyes, was a human chain of life - a living and breathing family tree. She rummaged in her bag and pulled out her phone.

'Uncle Rohan, I'm coming over,' she said, and jumped on a 176 bus.

*

Rohan Ramkishore lived alone in a tall, cream-coloured Victorian terrace house in South London. Bored with retirement, he had begun to renovate the old property. He had a smart new front door fitted and paid a builder to paint it black. He hung a large brass door knocker in the shape of a lion's head on it and added a matching letter box and keyhole. Then he instructed the builder to paint the edges of the sash windows in the same black paint. Aunt Sabby, his sister, who had lived next door before her death, hated what he had done to the house. The front door, she said, reminded her of a coffin and she accused him of bringing the neighbourhood down with his crass style. He laughed it off and cheekily offered her the services of his builder.

'So how did it go at the solicitor's? What did he tell you?' Uncle Rohan greeted his niece, opening the front door.

Uncle Rohan was a tall, handsome man, eighty-four years old and still as straight as a mop handle. His striking white hair remained thick and full of curls. He had a dark complexion and strong square shoulders - a result, he claimed, of pulling oxen up to the sugar factory in Trinidad when he was a boy. As a child, Indira had never believed him, because she hardly knew what an ox was.

'The solicitor said I have to prove who I am. What kind of nonsense is that, Uncle?' she said, shrugging off her coat.

'Don't worry with them,' he said, shuffling along the corridor in his slippers. 'These people love paperwork. They don't mind much what their clients do as long as they have it in writing. I'll make us some tea, while you go up to your Auntie's room and start looking through things.' He waved her up the stairs.

Indira put her foot on the first step and held on to the banister. She paused for a moment, staring at a framed photograph of her uncle as a young man, hanging on the wall. He looked fine and proud in his crisp white nurse's uniform. His hair was as black and shiny as his front door was now, and his long sideburns were clipped in line with his smiling mouth.

Rohan Ramkishore had arrived in London from Trinidad as a trainee in the 1960s, and number 47 Devonshire Road had been his home ever since. He only rented at first, living in one room on the first floor and saving every last penny he had to put down a deposit on a house. Aunt Sabby and the rest of the family came the following year, and when the house became vacant they clubbed together to buy the whole property. The purchase of number 49 a few years later was Aunt Sabby's idea, and soon brother and sister became a couple of local entrepreneurs, renting out rooms to newcomers from around the world.

'So, how's it going?' Uncle Rohan said, setting the tray down on Aunt Sabby's old bed. Indira heard the sadness in his voice.

'Ah, I still miss her too, Uncle,' she said holding his hands in hers.

'She was a wonderful lady,' he sighed. 'When she moved back in here so I could nurse her after she got sick, we became close all over again, just as we were when we were children back at home. I sat right here, on the edge of her bed, every night, talking of old stories. I miss that now,' he said, and he shook his head as if he could rattle the memory out of his mind.

Indira picked up a plastic box filled with papers and old photographs and fingered through them. Fishing out a handful of envelopes, she passed some to her uncle. They began opening them up one by one and setting the contents out on the floor. There were mostly bills and lots of old hire-purchase agreements for washing machines and a TV. Indira picked out the contract for the new central heating system.

'Remember this, Uncle?' she said. 'No more running across the road to Mr Stephens to buy a gallon of paraffin.' They laughed together.

'Those were tough times,' he agreed, opening another envelope. Then: 'Look at this,' he said, pointing to a photograph of Aunt Sabby.

It was a formal picture, taken at a studio with clouds running past her on the painted background. Her face was as round as the moon and flat - so that when she smiled, her cheeks popped out of the sides of her face like little red plums. On her wedding finger, she wore a large ruby ring studded with tiny diamonds. Although she had never married, Uncle Rohan and a substantial number in the community suspected that for all her life she had harboured the love of an unattainable man - probably a well-off Englishman, judging by the size of the ruby.

Reaching deep into the plastic box, Indira brought out another pile of envelopes. When one slipped from her fingers, Uncle Rohan snatched it from her lap.

'Now this is something!' he exclaimed. 'Look - it's your father's birth certificate.'

Indira took it from him and knelt to unfold it on the floor. Her knees clicked as she leaned forward. Tucking her feet beneath her, she sat back and read the certificate out loud.

Peter Ram Kishore, born 1932: Mountview Plantation, Trinidad and Tobago.

Indira got up and looked out of the window. The sky was ash-white with rainclouds and her heart felt as if a hundred rocks had been placed on her chest.

'I'm so confused,' she said, turning to her uncle. 'Was I adopted or something?' She retraced her childhood, taking long steps back in time. She hardly knew her father or her mother. Both had died in a car crash when she was a baby. All Indira knew about the accident was that she was thrown from the car by the impact and was lucky to be alive. She scanned the birth certificate again, peering at the old-fashioned handwriting, which was faded at the creases.

'So his father was also Kishore, and he was born in 1906, on the same plantation?' She felt Uncle Rohan's hand on her shoulder.

'Yes, that was your grandfather.'

Indira handed the document to her uncle and quietly walked back to the window.

'My grandfather,' she repeated bitterly. 'How can you call him that? My grandfather, my father, my uncle, my auntie . . . none of you are really my family. We have different names.'

Uncle Rohan came to stand beside her. They looked through the window together, staring down at Aunt Sabby's unkempt garden next door.

'Look at how wild her garden has become since she moved back in with me. And now she's gone, it's as if all the flowers and trees have given up hope, believing that nobody cares for them any more. But if you look carefully down there you can still see the vegetable beds she planted, the spinach and coriander she grew. Don't let the solicitor make you grow wild inside now that she has gone.'

He pointed to her father's birth certificate, saying, 'They are just names on pieces of paper, but you know who you are.'

Raising the lower half of the window, and before her uncle could stop her, Indira jumped down on to the flat roof, just like she used to as a child. Gingerly, she stepped over the low wall that separated the two houses at first-floor level, and peered through the skylight into her aunt's kitchen. Through the murk she saw pots still on the stove and, to the left, a long stainless-steel breadbin. It was the one that Indira had bought her more than ten years ago.

'Indira, come back!' her uncle shouted and disappeared from the window.

She didn't listen but slid slowly down the drainpipe of her aunt's kitchen wall. She tested the back door - locked - and then tried to ease open the kitchen window. She looked around for a stick, something to smash the window with.

'Indira, come back!' she heard her uncle call out to her again, this time over the garden fence. His worn-out fingers hung on to the top of the wooden boards as if he was trying to pull himself over. Suddenly, a set of keys flew through the air and landed on the patio by her feet.

'Open the French window,' she heard him say in a loud whisper.

The door was stuck. Indira heaved and pulled until it finally came loose. It opened - and a rush of stale air engulfed her; quickly, she covered her nose with the sleeve of her cardigan. She pushed back the heavy curtain and a pillar of light fell across the through-lounge, straight to the front window. The young woman waited a moment and then slowly entered the room, creeping like a burglar in the dead of night.

'Breaking and entering is a serious crime, my girl,' Uncle Rohan said breathlessly when he finally came through the adjoining gate and caught up with her. 'The solicitor will sue us.'

'I just want to collect the rest of my things,' she said. 'I should have done it years ago when I moved out. Don't worry, I'm not staying. The solicitor was right - I am a nobody.'

She felt Uncle Rohan slip his warm hand into hers. She tried to pull away at first but he squeezed tighter.

The house smelled musty. They wandered through the downstairs rooms, taking in the sadness of it all. Aunt Sabby's slippers in the hallway were still neatly paired; her favourite scarf still hung on the coat stand. The dining table and chairs, her grandfather clock, the chandeliers . . . all were trapped in a thick layer of dust. In the centre of the coffee table was a round crochet place mat. It looked like a huge dirty snowflake on frosted glass.

'She tried to teach me to crochet once, do you remember? I was all thumbs and no fingers,' Indira whispered to her uncle with a smile.

They drifted around the house, retracing Aunt Sabby's life and touching everything from little porcelain dolls on the mantelpiece to the pots and pans in the kitchen.

'Your Aunt Sabby could really cook. Smell that pot.' Uncle Rohan lifted the karahi to Indira's nose. 'You can still smell the curry powder,' he said wistfully. 'Do you want to take it?'

Indira grinned back at him. Her feelings of abandonment were leaving her. She felt that she belonged again.

Upstairs in Aunt Sabby's bedroom there was a square box made out of tiny cuts of glass and lined with red velvet. It was an Aladdin's Cave of pearl necklaces and rings with shiny colourful stones. Aunt Sabby loved costume jewellery and so did Indira. The two of them used to spend hours in the second-hand shops searching for hidden gems. Indira slipped a ring on her finger and admired the emerald-green stone against her skin.

'I gave her this for her birthday,' she said, and sat on her aunt's bed, raised her head to the ceiling and blinked back tears.

Uncle Rohan sat down beside her and stroked her head affectionately. After a few moments, he said, 'Come on. We can't stay for too long.'

Indira was about to follow him back down the stairs when she remembered the attic. 'Wait here, Uncle,' she said.

Upstairs in the attic, Indira felt as though she was disturbing the peace. She began rummaging through boxes and stacks of old newspapers, shifting sack after sack of black bags stuffed with moth-eaten clothes. Then she spotted it: a shoebox, size five, hidden under a broken plastic tub of marbles all the colours of the rainbow.

Crouching down, she scooped a handful of them into her palm, rolled them around and smiled to herself, remembering. She had won them at junior school. She recalled sitting by the drains in the playground, tipping her marbles with the side of a curled forefinger from one end of the dirty grate to the other. The game was eventually banned; the headmaster said it was unhygienic, sitting around playing with drains all day.

Reaching for a beam overhead, she hoisted herself up, holding the shoe box, and descended through the attic hatch. She hated the feeling of the dusty old box under her arm. Forty-five years of fallen hairs, dead skin and the withered wings of flies and wasps stuck to her clothes. To breathe in too deeply, she thought, would unsettle the tiny particles of grey matter that rested on the box lid. They would swirl up into her nostrils and become one with her body. To breathe out, however, would be worse. A deep sigh would unleash a whirlwind into the air, swirling about her face and clinging to her hair, eyebrows and red glossy lipstick.

Holding the box at arm's length, she trod carefully down the stairs to where her uncle was waiting for her.

Just then, they heard a car pull up outside. Indira lifted the front curtain just high enough to see the solicitor slamming his car door. He looked up and down the street and pulled out a set of keys. Indira and Uncle Rohan fled, back through the side gate and into his house. Breathless, they sped up to her aunt's room again. Uncle Rohan held his chest and sat on the bed, puffing loudly.

'Tell me, Uncle, I need to know. Am I family or not?' Indira said, handing him a notebook from the shoebox. She watched him flick through the pages.

'It's a long time since I saw this - I forgot you even had it,' he said. 'Come and sit next to me. Come, come,' he repeated, sliding off the bed and on to the floor.

It was a family tree, delicately written in a fine felt-tip pen. Indira looked at the paper closely and then at Uncle Rohan. She pulled her knees up to her face and rested her head on them, her arms wrapped closely around her legs as she waited.

Uncle Rohan took a sip of cold tea before announcing, 'Your aunt made this just after your father died. Look - you are at the top of this tree and your great-grandfather is at the bottom. You see here?'

Indira leaned over her uncle's shoulder and nodded her head.

'So, when your grandfather left Madras and went to Trinidad, those stupid people at the docks only registered his first name and spelled it wrong too; so instead of Kishoor Ramcharan, he became known as Kishore and his father's name was registered only as Ram, as if that was the family name. In those days, the British never called working people by their first names. Maybe they thought that if they did, they would have to treat us like human beings. I don't know why, but your grandfather became known around the plantation as Kishore. Now all the people he knew from back home called him Ram, his father's family name. You with me?'

He put his arms around Indira and hugged her. But she would not be distracted.

'Uncle, carry on,' she said, loosening her grip around her legs. She stretched them out and pointed her toes.

'So, time passed and your grandfather got married and had three children: me, your Aunt Sabby and your father Peter.'

Indira raised her head and looked at Uncle Rohan suspiciously. 'Hmm . . . so why was his name Peter? You all have Indian names, why was he different?' She was starting to sound like the solicitor.

Uncle Rohan laughed. 'OK, wait, so now your father was born and the midwife was a Christian woman and she liked everybody to be Christian, so before your grandfather could say a word, the woman named him Peter. It was no joke, Indira. We had no say in those days.'

'And then?' she prompted, trying to keep him on track.

'Look at the family tree,' he told her, pointing to the line with her father's name on it. 'You see how we all have the name Ram in front. That was your grandmother's doing. You could never mess with that lady, you know. She insisted the manager changed it. That's where you get your temper from,' Uncle Rohan said affectionately.

Indira beamed as she thought of her grandmother. She had never met her but had heard so much about her that she concluded she must have been a very fiery woman.

'So we move again. First India, then Trinidad and now England, and the mistakes carry on. You were the first born in this country and your mother went to the town hall with your aunt and asked the lady there to register your name. They called you

Clarence, after your grandmother - see here, look at the family tree - and Indira, because you were so beautiful. Now, this lady can't write Indian names, so she spelled Ramkishore how she wanted it, how the English say it. That's how you became Ramkeesoon. Maybe they didn't understand your mother's accent. Who knows, but you *are* one of us - and don't ever doubt it again.'

He gently pushed Indira from his shoulder and pinched her chin. 'Never!' he said with a wink.

A sudden knock on the front door brought both of them up on to their feet. Indira peeped out of the bedroom window.

'It's the solicitor,' she whispered.

They walked down the stairs slowly, holding hands, and opened the door wide.

'Good afternoon,' Indira heard her Uncle Rohan say in his most patronising voice. 'And you are . . .?'

Family Tree

Clarence Indira Ramkeesoon

daughter

Rohan Ramkishore   Peter Ram Kishore —— Chaaya Singh   Sabby Ramkishore

uncle   *father*   *mother*   *aunt*

Kishore —— Clarence

grandfather   *grandmother*

(formerly known as Kishoor Ram)

Ram —— Aditi

great-grandfather   *great-grandmother*

Sugar Cake

North London, 2005

THE STRING OF little Indian bells that hung on the back of the front door tinkled.

Mala was sitting at the dining table pouring brown sugar into an empty coffee mug. She needed one full cup to make Sugar Cake, and fortunately she had just about enough. The large crunchy granules sounded like a rain shower during monsoon in her tropical garden back home in British Guiana.

'Who the hell is that?' she called out, spilling the precious crystals on to the white cotton tablecloth. She eased herself out of her chair, and as quickly as an eighty-five-year-old could, she hobbled to the cooker and turned off the gas. The bubbling water eased in the pan and finally came to a stop.

The bells tinkled again. 'For goodness sake!' She threw up her arms and cried out, 'I'm coming!'

As she walked out into the hallway, she paused, holding on to the banister to catch her breath. Her eyes rested on the shadowy figure she saw through the frosted glass in the front door.

'Hello. Can I help you?' she asked, opening the door and leaning against it. A cool breeze pushed its way into the hallway, fanning her slightly sweaty face.

'Hello, Aunty,' the young man said. 'My name is David - I'm Alan's son.'

Stunned, Mala took a moment to shake off the numbness of shock that had crept into her body. She recognised the voice but not the man standing in front of her.

'Who?' she said shakily. 'Alan - who is he?' She rummaged around in her skirt pocket for her angina spray and pumped two short blasts into her mouth.

The young man smiled nervously, and bending down to meet her gaze, he whispered, 'You know - you called him Rockstar. I'm his son.'

The sound of her cousin's name seemed to lift her body right off the ground. 'Come in, come in,' she said, and, taking hold of his arm, she led him into the house.

As he stepped into the hallway, she eyed him from head to toe. He looked sharp in his dark blue suit and crisp white cotton shirt. Mala liked men to look smart and ladies to look glamorous; matching jewellery and polished shoes were the bare minimum she expected. If you wanted her respect, 'You had better learn to respect yourself,' as she used to say to her children when they were small.

He looked about forty, roughly the right age to be her cousin's son, but brown skin rarely aged quickly so he could easily have been ten years older. Her son and daughter had left her long ago to live in Canada; now it was only her grandchild, Esme, who flitted in and out of the house. The parcel tucked under the visitor's arm slipped as he paused to let Mala go in front of him - good manners, too. She was beginning to feel her old self again. 'Just take off your shoes and come in the dining room,' she instructed him, leading the way.

Her breathing had eased a little when she finally sat down. 'Sit, David, sit,' she puffed, patting the chair nearest to her. 'You gave me such a shock. It's been a *long* time since I saw your father, maybe fifty years.' She wrapped her hand around a gold-plated watch that had begun to feel tight on her wrist; agitatedly, she twisted it round and round. An old wound began to ache.

'How is he?' she asked.

'Aunty,' David pulled at the sticky tape on the brown package that he had placed on the table, 'I have some sad news to tell you.' He reached out and stilled her fidgeting hands. 'Daddy passed away six months ago.'

She pulled her hands free. Then shifted in her chair to ease the ache in her back. Her eyes focused on the tablecloth and the scattered crystals of brown sugar.

One by one she pressed them with the tip of her forefinger; they stuck to her and she brushed them off back into the cup.

'I hate to waste,' she said, looking up at David with an awkward smile. She coughed a deep chesty cough and slid her hand on the table, palm side up, towards him. In the quiet that followed, Mala fought back tears. Reaching for the roll of kitchen towel in the middle of the table, she ripped off a sheet, folded it into two and tore it in half. She put one half on the table and buried her eyes in the other.

'Cancer?' she asked in a muffled voice.

'No, Aunty, it was his liver.'

As he spoke, she pressed down on the kitchen towel harder until her eyes hurt. They were bloodshot when she finally opened them.

'He wanted me to give you this.'

As David pushed the brown paper package towards her, the little Indian bells tinkled again.

'That door! It'll be the death of me,' Mala grumbled shakily as she reached for the back of her chair to pull herself up.

Then she added: 'In spite of everything, Rockstar was always my favourite cousin, you know.' Her voice was warm now and she was smiling down at David. She dabbed at her eyes again. 'Do you know how he got the nickname, Rockstar?' she asked, but didn't wait for the young man to reply. 'He thought he could sing. Even when he was small, he thought he was the best singer in the whole village. But he couldn't even hum in tune, let alone sing. He was terrible! We never told him, though. That's bad - right?'

They laughed for a moment until the bell tinkled again.

'Give me strength.' Mala gritted her teeth and plodded down the hall to open the front door. 'I'm coming, I'm coming! I'm a pensioner, you know,' she yelled at the shadow in the doorway.

'I'm sorry, Grandma, I left my keys at work.' It was Esme. She barged into the house, looking at her phone. Bending down, she pecked her grandmother automatically on the cheek and without looking up said, 'I'm not stopping,' and kicked off her sandals in the hallway. 'I just came back to pick up my purse - forgot it was in my other handbag.'

Walking towards the dining room, she suddenly stopped, turned around and pointed to the unknown pair of shoes next to hers. *'Whose are they?'* she mouthed as though her grandmother was hard of hearing.

Esme had warned Mala not to let anyone into the house while she was alone, but the old lady never listened. Sometimes, Esme would come home to find her sitting quietly watching TV with a total stranger next to her on the sofa. One day, there were two tourists seated at the dining table. They were looking at a map of London, trying to find out how to get to

St Paul's Cathedral from Tottenham High Road. Mala had even made them tea. Esme had to shoo them out like a couple of stray cats.

'I hate sitting here alone all day, watching the tap drip,' Mala would say. The tap dripping was a dig at her granddaughter, who had promised to fix it some weeks ago. The house was falling apart since Mala had retired twenty years earlier, and with so many things to do and so little money, a dripping tap was hardly a priority.

'Can I help you?' Esme enquired suspiciously as she popped her head around the dining-room door.

David stood up and put out his hand. 'Hello, I'm David. Aunty Mala was my dad's cousin.'

'I'm Esme, nice to meet you. Grandma never mentioned . . .' She heard her grandmother sigh.

'Your uncle has died, Esme. Come and sit down.' Mala shuffled along to make room for Esme at the table.

'I'm sorry, Grandma, I can't - I have to run.' Esme was checking her texts as she spoke.

Mala glared at her. 'Then at least make the boy some tea,' she ordered.

'Grandma, are you all right?' Esme bent down to look her in the face, noticing for the first time that she seemed flustered. 'OK, OK, I'll make you both some tea, and then I'll go.'

Mala's stomach grumbled, and, pushing the parcel to one side, she picked up a packet of greaseproof cake cases and stared at the label. 'I was going to make some Sugar Cake when you knocked,' she told her visitor. 'Would you like some?'

David didn't hesitate. 'Yes, please. I haven't had Sugar Cake in years.' He rubbed his belly and joked: 'I'll start my diet next week.'

Esme brought the freshly made tea to the table and pushed the sugar bowl in front of him, saying, 'A little sugar won't kill you - and, of course, we only do brown sugar in this house. Demerara - the best.' She winked at David and handed him a teaspoon. 'Help yourself; it's better for you than the white stuff.' Then she muttered awkwardly, 'Look, I'm so sorry about your dad,' trying to sound sympathetic, but when the phone in her pocket buzzed, she said, 'I have to go back to work, Grandma.'

Mala didn't even bother to look up. She had become used to these fleeting visits. Even though Esme lived at home, her granddaughter pretty much treated the place like a hotel, breezing in and out when she felt like it.

'Don't forget, I'm locking the door at ten-thirty,' Mala called out. 'If you're not home by then, you will have to sleep somewhere else.' But the front door slammed while she was still speaking.

'The little devil,' she said, smiling at David. 'At least we can have some peace now. OK, let me get this Sugar Cake on the go.' And forgetting her tea, she rolled forward, clutching her knees as she pushed herself up.

'Aunty, I know you and Dad fell out.' David felt a little bolder now that Esme was out of the house, but Mala was already standing at the cooker.

'Come over, son, and bring the sugar with you,' she said, lighting the gas ring under the pan of water.

Maya had intended to gather the rest of the ingredients from the dining table, but instead she marched across to the end of the kitchen. David, who was by now setting the mug of sugar on the kitchen counter, froze as he watched Mala reach behind the pedal bin and pull out a sheath made up of old newspapers.

'Do you know what this is?' Mala was taunting him. The yellowing paper fell to the floor as she carefully withdrew a long, shiny blade. 'This cutlass has been with me for more than fifty years. It was my father's and for years he used it to cut sugar cane.' Mala paused. 'There was a time when I wanted to use it myself. Your dad had a lucky escape.' She plucked at the blade. 'Look, it's still sharp.' And she took a step forward, saying mischievously, 'Do you want to test it?'

'Aunty!' David shouted out, beginning to perspire, but she hadn't finished her moment in the limelight yet.

Picking up a coconut from the kitchen counter, she boasted, 'Watch this,' as she placed a Pyrex bowl in the sink. Cupping the coconut in the palm of her left hand, she lifted the heavy blade slowly in her right and tapped on its hard, dark brown shell. Then, closing one eye, she scored an imaginary line on the rough hairy surface of the nut and tossed it lightly in the air. She caught it, steadied herself one more time and then tossed it again.

Cutlass at the ready, Mala caught the coconut and gave it a short sharp chop. 'Aha! Still got it,' she giggled, and repeated the action several times, each time throwing the nut slightly forward so the cut travelled all the way around. Then she heard a crack, followed by a hollow sound as the coconut split and fresh coconut water gushed out into the bowl below. She wrenched the coconut open with the blade and put the cutlass down.

She felt a sense of liberation. 'It's been a long time since I did that!' she beamed, and puffed out her chest proudly. 'I'm slower now, though. In the old days, Rockstar and I could cut coconuts from a whole palm tree in the time that I can cut one now.'

She handed the pieces of coconut over to David. 'Now, can you grate it?'

*

Mala tipped the cup of brown sugar into the boiling water and added half a teaspoon of vanilla extract and a cinnamon stick to the pan. She let it boil, swishing the liquid around until the mixture was reduced to a thick syrup, like molten lava. Then she added the grated coconut and a teaspoon of fresh ginger, turning the ingredients over and over until the coconut was fully coated. Taking a tablespoon, she scooped up sugary mounds one by one and dropped them into a line of cake cases. Then she left them on the kitchen counter to set.

*

'The doctor told me to cut down on my sugar, but I don't pay him any attention.' Mala had a broad smile on her face as she peeled away tiny strips of greaseproof paper that had stuck to the Sugar Cake. She took a bite of the first one to test it, examining its soft centre, and then placed one on David's plate. Stretching over to the brown parcel, she dragged it towards her.

'What is it in here that you want me to see, son?' She stared at the parcel. 'Do you know what is inside?'

David took a bite of his Sugar Cake and nodded with his mouth full.

'Then why don't you just tell me?' Her lips quivered. Sitting back on her chair, Mala held her wrist again. The watch felt tight; it began to irritate her and so she released the clasp and let it slide from her hand on to the table.

'Rockstar was a difficult man when he was young,' she said. She smoothed out the tablecloth, scooping up the coconut crumbs and returning them to her plate. 'He used to drink a lot. They worked so hard back home, we all did, but the men seemed to suffer the most. Cutting sugar cane all day in the hot sun can do something to the brain, you know?' She looked at David, drawing his attention to the cutlass leaning against the wall in the kitchen. 'That cutlass alone used to cut a tonne of cane a day - a day, my boy! Can you imagine that?'

Reaching out to him, she held his hand, turning it over so that she could see the lines in his palm. She traced them with her fingers. 'So soft . . .,' she whispered.

Then, more sombrely: 'The rum shops in Albion did a roaring trade.' Mala let go of his hand and popped a coconut crumb into her mouth. 'Your father was a very good customer, but when he stole from me to pay his drinking debts, I just couldn't forgive him. It all seems so petty now.' She unconsciously rubbed her wrist.

'It was the night before my wedding. My mother had given me a beautiful gold bangle, thick and decorated with so many fine cuts that it glistened in the moonlight. One minute it was on my table wrapped up in tissue and then the next it was gone. I never saw it again.' She wiped away a tear and said in a voice hoarse with emotion: 'It is a terrible thing, addiction.'

She sat for a moment, studying David. 'You know, you sound just like your father when you speak. It feels as if he's right here in the room.'

'Aunty, he was sorry - did you know that? He was a drunk man, it's true, but you can't blame him, Aunty. There were too many debts to pay. Every Saturday, after he cut cane for the whole week, he would go to the moneylender to pay off his debts; he'd give the man the money and then take out a new loan. Instead of getting smaller, the debts just grew bigger. I was only a baby and then my sister came along, and all the time, the debts mounted up.'

Mala's eyes widened. 'Is that what he told you? He had to steal my bangle to feed his children! No, son. He was a drunk and he spent all his money in the rum shop, that's what happened - it's as simple as that. Do you know how I suffered because of him? Your grandmother, God rest her soul, never forgave me! Me!'

Mala's face burned as she recalled that night. 'She blamed me for everything.'

'Aunty, can't you forgive him? Open the parcel, please.' The young man pushed it towards her.

Mala took a glance at David. Placing her hand on her chest, she pressed down hard as if she could somehow stop her heart from hurting inside. He pushed the parcel closer, and tears welled up in her eyes. Boom - there it was again: her heart reverberating with the remembered pain of the past.

David persisted. Suddenly, she snatched up the parcel and ripped off the strip of sticky tape, knocking over the plate piled with Sugar Cakes. They scattered like bowling pins, spinning across the table. She shook the parcel frantically; a single item rolled out and clinked against her plate. It sparkled and glistened like a thousand tiny golden stars.

The little Indian bells tinkled in the hallway. David stood up.

'Leave it,' Mala whispered, still staring at the bangle. 'Leave it and sit down.' She picked up the remaining strip of kitchen towel and pressed it down hard on her eyes, wiping away tears.

'I want to hear more about Rockstar.'

Sugar Cake

Sugar Cake is a delightfully simple, additive-free recipe. This is my low-sugar version for those of you who want to cut down on the sweet stuff.

Ingredients
1 grated coconut
2oz Demerara sugar
8oz water
1 cinnamon stick or teaspoon of grated nutmeg
1/2 teaspoon of vanilla extract
1 teaspoon freshly grated ginger

Method

First take a hammer (not a cutlass!) and break open the hard shell of the coconut. Remember to hold it over a bowl so that you can catch the coconut water as it trickles through the shell. Set the coconut water to one side and grate the flesh of the coconut, coarsely or finely according to your preference. Lightly toast the grated coconut by turning it over and over in a pan on a low heat so that it doesn't burn. Set to one side.

Pour 8 fluid ounces of water into a pan; add 3 ounces of sugar and stir over a low heat until the sugar dissolves. Add the grated ginger, one cinnamon stick or grated nutmeg and half a teaspoon of vanilla extract. Stir the sugar water until the mixture reduces into a thick silky syrup. Remove the cinnamon stick. Add the grated coconut and stir over a low heat until it is completely covered with the syrup. Keep stirring for 2-3 minutes and then turn off the heat.

On greaseproof paper spoon out mounds of Sugar Cake and allow to set.

Drink the coconut water.

Home

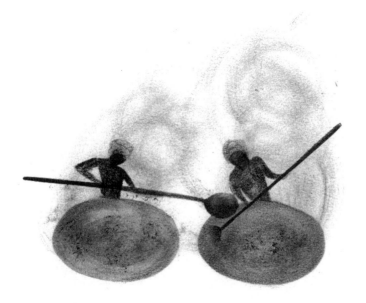

Fiji, 1896

WHEN BIDHOO TOLD me he was leaving, I was sitting on my bunk cross-legged, feeling for fresh wounds on my skin. The two below my knee didn't worry me, but the third - just above my ankle - had become infected. It burned unbearably and it had started to swell.

Bidhoo had caused the accident, but he was not the one to blame. His temper had got the better of him, that's all. He was a good man, the only one who treated me with kindness and respect.

'Ranghee, you are like a father to me,' he would say when I scolded him for talking back to the Sirdars. They were dangerous Indians who were appointed by the managers to keep watch over us.

Perhaps his mind was already on a ship and had left the island. We had a few weeks to wait for our papers that would release us from this place. Why Bidhoo believed the manager would stand by his word and return them I will never know. I myself knew it was hopeless. Our labour was worth more to them than honouring our contracts. And the manager was not an honourable man. Bidhoo needed those papers to board the ship that would take him home. Without them, he would be like a fugitive living a life on the run.

Five years is a long time to wait to see your family again. It was what had kept Bidhoo alive.

But sometimes false hope is worse than no hope at all.

We were working side by side creaming scum off boiling sugar-cane juice. The syrup bubbled and spat at us from huge copper pots. All day we dipped, lifted and poured the sweet steaming sugar water from one pot to another. The giant ladles in our hands grew heavier and heavier as the day went on. By the end of our shift we were exhausted. That was when the Sirdar walked up to Bidhoo and tapped him on the shoulder with a long baton. Bidhoo should have known that the manager would send the Sirdar to taunt him.

'Bidhoo,' he said boldly. 'The manager said he won't let you go.' And then he laughed so loudly that his voice bellowed around the factory floor. His belly was fat and round, and he rubbed it as though he had just eaten a heavy meal before waving the baton vigorously from side to side in Bidhoo's face.

'If you don't sign up for another five years, you will be back out there in the fields. They'll make you work twice as hard and cut twenty chains of cane a day.' He said it louder the second time, goading my friend to react. Bidhoo's face turned red. He threw the ladle down to the ground and pushed the Sirdar once - and then again.

The Sirdar stood firm. 'You will never leave here, never.' He prodded Bidhoo's arm with his stick.

This time, Bidhoo snapped. He swung at the Sirdar; the two men fell to the ground and started punching each other. In his fury, Bidhoo accidentally pushed me and I slashed my leg open on the rough edge of the copper pot. As I rose, my hand cupping the wound which was gushing with blood, the Sirdar ran out of the factory.

That night, the Sirdar followed us home. In the darkness, he danced alongside us, twisting and turning like an evil spirit around our weary bodies. Mischievously he played with our minds, trying to sow seeds of doubt and despair. I felt a sense of relief when I saw the huts in the distance and the reassuring trails of smoke from a camp fire in the small clearing outside. I nudged Bidhoo to warn him not to react, and we walked faster. Cheated of his prey, as we neared the huts the Sirdar jumped in front of us and jabbed at us both this time, shouting out his terrible threats.

'So, do you still believe you are going home, Bidhoo?' He sniggered loudly and then suddenly lowered his voice. 'The only place you are going to is prison,' he said, and he prodded Bidhoo so that he stumbled backwards. 'I can keep you out, but it will come at a price.'

He paused and hissed, 'I want two shillings by tomorrow, otherwise I'll tell the manager that you assaulted me - and you'll be locked up. I'll make sure of it!'

I tried to block out the Sirdar's voice. Had I been a braver man I would have fought him there and then, just as Bidhoo had. But I was not like Bidhoo at all. I was a timid fellow, a coward, and I bowed my head and promised that we would have the money.

'Make sure you do,' he said, and with his baton he hit my leg, aiming deliberately at my wound. The cut started to bleed again.

Bidhoo, unlike me, found it difficult to adjust to life on the plantation. The work, we had discovered, was far harder than we all expected. We woke up at four in the morning and sometimes finished at six at night. He checked his contract several times.

'It's nine hours a day, not eleven,' he protested when the overseer patrolled the cane fields.

Eventually we were moved to factory work, which was supposed to be less physical. It was a promotion of sorts although it never felt that way. Worst of all was when the manager charged us more for our rations and during the busy harvest sometimes forced us to work on Sundays, our only day off.

'This is no life at all,' Bidhoo had protested.

It was all right for me. My dreams had evaporated like overnight rain when the sun rose on the very first day we ended our voyage from Calcutta and anchored off Fiji, sick and exhausted. It is hard, when I think back on it, to believe that my dreams ever existed. If I became passive it was because I wanted to survive; in contrast, Bidhoo's fiery spirit just grew stronger. That was his downfall.

*

The first time I met Bidhoo, he was standing on deck looking out towards a cloudless sky. He was tall and handsome, not short and round like me, and when he spoke his voice boomed about like a cannonball. We were strangers then, brought together on rough seas, and if we began our journey in high spirits, by the time we arrived at our destination, mine had sunk to the bottom of the great black sea, the Kala Pani . . . the dark waters of no return . . . where they still lie.

We lived in a long, barrack-like building with a slanted tin roof; it was situated but a short walk from the factory. The place was divided into 'rooms' by threadbare curtains that hung from strips of woven gauze wire attached to the ceiling. It was the poor man's ventilation that was supposed to allow fresh, clean air to drift along through the rooms and clear out the stale air. Without it, forty people or more would easily suffocate in their sleep at night.

Our 'room' was a dismal place. Pushed up against one wall were three double bunks, while on the other, eight cutlasses were lined up like warriors. Firewood in the corner fed a stove blackened with soot. Dirty pots and pans were strewn across the floor. Eight men slept there at night - six on the bunks and two on the floor. Bidhoo's bunk was next to mine.

Evenings were lively affairs. As the workers returned, the noise increased, and by nightfall the building breathed chaos. There was no privacy here. Most of the workers liked to eat outside where the air was fresher and cooler. Usually, we joined them - but not on this particular night, after the fight with the Sirdar. We needed to talk.

'How much money have you got?' I asked Bidhoo in a low voice. He pulled away when I touched the bruise on his face. His black eye was still closed. I offered him the food on my plate but he refused. It was no wonder - the roti flatbread was cold and hard and the dhal and rice were lukewarm in my mouth. Hunger rumbled in my belly. I took another mouthful and swallowed quickly.

'Ranghee,' Bidhoo said softly, 'I will not pay him, and neither will you. I'd rather kill him.'

My body shivered at the thought.

'If what the Sirdar says is true and the manager does not give me my papers,' he went on, 'I will not stay. I'll go on the run.'

'I can pay,' I volunteered. 'I have some savings. It is a dowry for my daughter.'

The money, five shillings and three pennies, had taken me more than a year to save. That was the last time I saw Nelum. She told me that she had met a boy. He worked as a stable-hand just behind the manager's house where she was employed as a domestic servant. Bidhoo had been my first choice for her, but not any more. Not everyone was as keen to go back to India as he was.

I stamped on a line of ants that swarmed around my food and the draught from this lifted the curtain, exposing two feet. The toes were pointing towards our room. The Sirdar was eavesdropping. Bidhoo threw a large pot at him and he dashed out of the hut.

'Ranghee, he will never leave us alone,' Bidhoo said urgently. 'Today you pay, tomorrow he will be back and the next day and the next - and so it will go on. I am an honest man. I work hard and have done my time here. My contract is over but I am warning you, if the manager will not give me my papers, then I will leave while I am still a free man.'

He lay down on his bunk and turned his back to me. Restless, unable to sleep, we stared at the ceiling. Dusk moved in. It did not take long for the night-time creatures to fan out across the floor. A low light glowed from the stove; the fire was almost burned out. Soon the other men would join us.

Bidhoo lowered his voice as if he wanted to tell me a secret. 'Last night,' he said, 'I saw my mother in my dreams. She was lying in her bed and called my name. I saw her reach out her hands to the empty space beside her bed. The room was bare and she was in darkness.' He paused and swallowed, and I imagined his tearful eyes.

'I used to light a candle by her bed every night, Ranghee. What if she is dying? I cannot wait another day. I must see her again. I shall go - but not without your blessing.'

His words fell from his mouth so calmly, but he must have known I couldn't give him what he wanted. He would be a deserter, destined to live in the bush as a scavenger, far away from the people he loved.

'Bidhoo,' I murmured, 'you are not destined to die here. You are like a son to me - you must live. If you believe that my blessing will set you free, you are wrong. The opposite will happen, my friend. It will put you in a prison for life. You must wait. The manager will give you your papers, I am sure of it. Your contract is served and you will be free to come and go as you please.'

I closed my eyes and willed my words to be true. I tried to dredge my hopes back up from the seabed, but they slipped down again like a sunken ship. Bidhoo's words filled the vacant spaces in my head and I remembered my mother, father and wife. Their faces flew at me like swooping birds and I was helpless, so lonely. I longed to see them one more time. When they died in the famine, I too died inside - but my legs kept moving. On and on I walked with my child in my arms towards the docks in the dust and the heat. We walked forward, never looking back.

'Ranghee, if you cannot give me your blessing then come with me. Come with me, please. I cannot do this on my own.'

'Bidhoo,' I pleaded, 'give me one last chance before you decide. Let me help you. Promise me that you will wait - and if I fail, then I will give you my blessing. Freedom will come to you, Bidhoo. Just a few weeks more. I beg you.'

There was a moment of silence. And then: 'One more chance,' he said, and closed his eyes.

*

Later that night, the Sirdar returned. Like a cockroach he scuttled across to my bunk and slapped his hand across my mouth to cut off my cry. I struggled down from the bed and he led me out of the room.

'The money,' he growled at me. His eyes were red and wild.

My body was heavy from sleep and I could barely stand upright. He spun me around and pushed me out of the hut, down towards the river bank. He was agitated, constantly turning around to look back at the house, to check whether we were being watched.

'What do you want from me?' I said, finally alert.

Cold water swirled around my feet, stinging my ankle. The wound opened up again and for a brief moment I thought back to the fight on the factory floor. A surge of hatred filled me and I lunged at him, but he was faster than me.

'I want your money,' he said. He followed me further into the water. 'You have a dowry for your daughter. Tell me where it is.'

I went for him again - but backed away immediately, arms outstretched, when he took out a knife and waved it at me. 'Where is it?' he hissed.

He waded in after me and we moved further and further out towards the middle of the river until we were just an arm's length apart. And then - without warning - I dived underwater, seized his legs and dragged him beneath the surface. He was strong, but that did not save him. He thrashed about, but I did not let go. I pulled him down deeper and shook him violently, with all of my strength. He twisted and turned, desperately trying to loosen my grip. My lungs burned. Then he suddenly stopped moving. I saw his knife sink to the bottom of the river.

I swam to the surface and frantically heaved in gulps of air. It took a moment before he floated to the top to join me. Grabbing hold of the body, I pushed it downstream, well away from the scene of the drowning.

A single cloud drifted across the moon, plunging the river into darkness as I silently swam back to the river bank. A sudden knocking sound distracted me. With long strokes, I followed it and found, just a few feet away from where we had entered the water, a small canoe tied to an overhanging branch. I clung on to the side, digging my nails into the wood, and pulled myself in - first my right leg and then my left - and I tumbled down low on to the deck. The boat swayed from side to side and nudged against the bank.

Then I heard a familiar voice, calling me from the river bank. It was Bidhoo. I pushed the boat away from the shore and paddled over to him.

The cloud drifted free from a moonbeam, which lit up the river. Thousands of shimmering stars spun around and dazzled my eyes. I felt alive, reborn. I prayed for my daughter, my family - and for the first time, for Bidhoo. He waded out to meet me, and hoisted himself into the canoe.

'Let us go to the sea,' I said, smiling broadly.

His face was as bright as the moon and we began to row.

We turned our backs to the cane fields that lined the river banks to the right of us, and wondered at the glorious lush and green mountains on the other side. We breathed in the fresh air and drank the clear water until we were ready to burst. Fish swam in every direction and there was quiet except for the lazy sound of waves lapping the edge of our boat. We passed the dead body of the Sirdar, washed up on the bank. We were fugitives now.

When we reached the mouth of the river we moored our boat in a secluded place and ran as fast as we could up the side of the sandy bank. The sun was still rising and the deep yellow sky with streaks of red and orange was breathtaking. Fine sand stuck to my toes as I raced along behind Bidhoo.

Suddenly, he stopped by a coconut tree. Breathless, I rested beneath it while he wrapped his legs around the trunk and started to ascend. I held my hand up to my eyes to watch his silhouette scramble to the top like a black spider. And then he sat there, swaying like a lookout perched on the mast of a ship, creaking from side to side in the swirling wind. I saw him stretch out his hand as if to capture the rising sun.

There was a ship out there, anchored in the bay and casting a shadow across the glistening water. Once upon a time, the great Kala Pani had engulfed my dreams and dragged them to the bottom of the seabed. Now it had released them - and as they rose to the surface, I knew that I would be home again soon.

The Tin Ticket

Mauritius, present day

THE DISCOVERY OF the tin ticket had made the morning news on the TV. The reporter, a rookie with the Mauritius Daily, had called the news desk the moment he found it, lying like a burnt-out fire cracker under a pile of bricks at the base of a disused chimney stack.

'The owner of this tin ticket may be a mystery . . .,' he said, excitedly holding up the metal tube to the camera, '. . . but what is clear is that the site of this old sugar mill has many more secrets to surrender.'

Laxmi had just finished plaiting her hair when she saw him brandishing the tin ticket. His eyes looked wild, as if he'd found Lord Krishna himself. She immediately set down her hairbrush and rushed out of the house, heading towards the derelict sugar mill. Half-walking, half-running, she felt in the rucksack over her shoulder, checking for the sharp edges of a garden trowel.

'Hey, Laxmi!' a shrill voice called at her from a salmon-coloured verandah halfway down the street. 'Have you seen the news?'

It was her best friend Anju, but Laxmi did not stop.

'I'm going there now!' she shouted back, nervously clicking her fingers. It was a habit that she had learned from her father when he was alive. 'It's a smart man's way to stay calm when things get on top of you,' he used to say when the pressures of life became too much.

Laxmi, a waitress at the Sugar Loaf Hotel and Spa, and self-appointed custodian of the collective village memory, had vowed to protect its secrets since childhood. She had begun burying family heirlooms in the grounds of the old sugar mill the year that a terrible cyclone ripped through Sun Street, tearing up their homes like flimsy strips of paper. She didn't know what a tin ticket was at first. The item had fallen from the eaves of the roof, which had cracked and splintered in the battering winds. Her child's instinct told her it was important and, just as her mother rushed her out of the house, she snatched it off the ground and hid it behind her back.

From that day, Laxmi scoured Sun Street for relics of the past, patiently overturning rocks and stones and checking the hollowed-out trunks of ancient trees. And when she didn't find them in the street, she turned to the homes of her friends, neighbours and family.

'It means something to all of us this way,' Laxmi had pleaded with her mother the day she was caught placing an old photograph of her grandfather into an empty tobacco tin. Her mother, beautiful yet stern, had scolded her as she pressed out the folds that now criss-crossed her father's face.

'It is not yours to take,' she said, fixing the picture back into its frame. She warned Laxmi never to return to the mill.

That was when the night visits began. Every Sunday when the tops of the coconut palms shimmered in the bright moonlight, Laxmi would lower the relics of her Indian past gently, ceremoniously, into the brittle earth - a rusty old tiffin, an oil lamp, the tin ticket, bells, bracelets, clay pots. She had scattered them all around the grounds of the mill.

The clicking of heels behind her clambered over Laxmi's thoughts. It was Anju.

'Slow down, slow down,' her friend panted.

Anju was the flamboyant type and too loud for such a short and skinny frame. Exceptionally nosy, she was aware of every single birth, death, marriage, engagement and affair on Sun Street. Strange to think that for all her observations, she never noticed Laxmi sneak away two tiny cymbals, tied together by a short thread, the day Anju's great-grandfather was cremated. He was a great musician with a voice like the gods, the family said at his funeral. As for Laxmi, she was becoming an accomplished thief.

'Who do you think it belongs to?' Anju said when she had caught up.

'Us,' Laxmi replied boldly. She left Anju standing in the street dumbfounded and hurried on towards the sugar mill.

At the end of Sun Street, she turned left down Robert Road, named after the first British Governor of Mauritius. She revelled in the signs of her past, good and bad. Rue de Soleil, as it used to be called, was originally named by the French, more than two centuries ago. They claimed it was the first place the sun's rays kissed the island. When the British came, they translated it as Sun Street, although for Laxmi there was nothing sunny about it. For Sun Street had once been the epicentre of a cholera outbreak that had taken the lives of hundreds of labourers.

Dodging a dazzling display of pink flowers, she crossed the road to avoid giant fruit bats gorging themselves on the orange-yellow flesh of the jackfruit. The leaves shook violently and the bats, as black as night, lurched into the air, momentarily blocking out the sun like a thick rain cloud.

'Still scared of them?' Baba, a street-seller, teased her from behind an old, disused wooden cart laden with fresh green coconuts. The cart's enormous wheels, shoulder-high, had been smartened up with a fresh coat of bottle-green paint. It used to ferry cut cane to the mill. If only, Laxmi thought as she hurried past, she could bury that!

When she eventually made it to the old sugar mill, she found the reporter kneeling down at the foot of the chimney stack, dragging up dust with his pen. He was taller and thinner than he looked on television, more handsome in the flesh. His rolled-up shirt sleeves revealed muscular arms. A brown leather satchel lay on the ground beside him.

'Is that where you found it?' she asked, feigning curiosity as she bent down quietly beside him. A chain with a gold locket dangled from his neck, catching the sunlight.

'One minute,' he said, blowing dust from his pen. Like a priest holding an open Bible at a sermon, he scribbled in his notebook while Laxmi clicked her fingers impatiently. He jotted down:

For more than one hundred years this chimney has cast a shadow over the village, here in Belle Mar.

'An interesting choice of words,' she said, peering at the page over his shoulder. 'There are no shadows here.'

'Aren't there?' He turned to face Laxmi. 'There are always shadows - the stories that people would rather you did not hear.'

'Where's the tin ticket?' she asked. The piercing in his ear surprised her. He was younger than she thought.

He handed it to her reverently and steadied his notebook again, his pen poised over the page.

'Who do you think it belonged to?' he wanted to know, and waited for her reply.

There was a long pause.

Then: 'Belongs to,' Laxmi corrected him. She never used the past tense when speaking about her ancestors. To her, the latter were still alive - not breathing in the same way that living beings do, but living on in the memories of the people she saw as she went about her business every day.

In Laxmi's underground collection, it was the tin ticket that was the most precious. It had hung around her great-grandmother's neck when she had travelled hundreds of miles from India to the island. It contained a contract. Five years she was to stay on the island working on the plantation. Rumour had it that she had tried to rebel and return to India early, but the truth never came out.

Laxmi cast her eyes around the grounds of the old sugar mill as she perched on the edge of a low brick wall that outlined the former factory floor. Under the earth she pictured a small clay pot belonging to Baba's grandmother. A tooth belonging to her grandfather lay in a dark corner under the ancient jacaranda tree where the flowers fell in winter. The cymbals belonging to Anju's great-grandfather were buried right under her feet.

The reporter sat beside her, his pen at the ready. 'Are you saying that you believe in ghosts?' He jotted down notes, smiling and shaking his head as if to mock her.

'I bet you'd like to say that. I'm not some dumb crazy kid, you know.' Laxmi jumped off the wall and stepped gingerly over to the jacaranda tree, now in full bloom with purple flowers. Perhaps he had a point. Would anyone in their right mind steal from their neighbours and bury their belongings in the ground? Then there were the notes. 'Letters to the dead', she called them. Her way of telling her ancestors that their sacrifices were not in vain.

Deba has gone to university. Manju has given birth to her third child. Sarah has converted to Christianity. Manoj has left us for England. Anju got married last year. Her husband bought her a gold bangle and stud nose ring for her birthday.

There was a system to Laxmi's project. She had laid out a plan of the sugar mill on the back of a discarded poster advertising pure brown sugar that she had found lying on the ground one day on her way to work.

She sketched out the chimney, she drew the arched walls of blue basalt stone. An x marked the spot where she had hidden away each precious item. She was creating a legacy, thirty feet by fifty feet long.

Just then, a car pulled up in the clearing and a man, his round belly bursting the buttons of his shirt, called over to the reporter.

'Where do you want me to start?' he said, closing the car door behind him.

Laxmi watched as the two men shook hands energetically, turning the tin ticket in her hand. They exchanged words and then walked towards her.

'This is Mr Gopal, an eminent historian from Port Louis,' the reporter said, pointing to his companion. His cream-coloured suit reminded Laxmi of a hospital porter. 'He's come to look around, to see if he can find any more artefacts. This is . . .'

There was a pause as both men waited for a reply.

'Laxmi,' she obliged.

'Ah, and who does this beautiful specimen belong to?' Mr Gopal said, reaching for the tin ticket. Laxmi reluctantly handed it over.

'I haven't seen one like this in years - and you say there are more items like this here?' He looked around the old site. 'It's a most unusual find. These mills have been out of action for a long time. They used to be the heart of the community until the price of sugar fell and the British abandoned them.'

He set the tin ticket gently on the ground and bent down at the base of the chimney stack, shifting rocks and stones out of the way.

'It was here, you say? How strange.' He pulled at the dust with his hands, carefully piling it up till it peaked like a jagged grey mountain. His head disappeared into the chimney breast.

Laxmi's nerves twisted and tightened in her head. She began to click her fingers.

Unexpectedly, Mr Gopal retreated from the chimney breast and sat back on his knees.

'I should have brought my tools,' he said, looking over at the reporter.

'OK, let's go and get them.' The young man turned to Laxmi. 'Coming?'

Laxmi shook her head. 'Thanks, but I need to get back to work.'

*

The walk back from the old sugar mill dragged on. Laxmi stared at her shoes, dusty on the tips, and imagined Anju setting out tables in the restaurant ready for the lunchtime rush. She pictured the disbelief on her manager's face when he learned that she'd be late in today; her excuses were never that convincing. None of that mattered now, though. There was much more at stake.

Crossing the main road, a bus loaded with tourists slowed down alongside her. They peered out of the window taking photographs as though she was part of a living museum.

When she reached Robert Road she was surprised to see the reporter leaning on his car, the engine still running. Mr Gopal was in the passenger seat.

'Let me at least give you a lift to work,' the reporter said, offering her his hand.

'I'm OK,' she told him, watching Mr Gopal through the window.

'Come back later then, after work,' he persisted. 'I'd like to do an interview.'

'Later?' she said in a daze. 'How long will you be gone?'

'About an hour, if there's not too much traffic. Come on, Laxmi,' he coaxed. 'You'll be famous.'

To be famous was the last thing that Laxmi wanted.

'I'll think about it,' she said, desperate to get rid of him. As the car disappeared around the bend, Laxmi stood still, listening to the fading sound of its engine. When she was sure that the car had gone, she dashed back to the mill.

Bolting up the stairs to the chimney stack, she lay on her back and slid her way into the chimney breast head first. Crumbling debris trickled on to her face as she loosened an old sugar sack from its inner wall. Spitting off the dust that clung to her lips, she wiggled backwards out of the dark cavern, sat up in the open air and grappled with its contents as the bag split.

'Rats!' She screamed, pulling her fists to her mouth to muffle her terrified sounds. She pushed her hand through the bottom of the sack. Fraying threads looped around her fingers.

'That's how they found it!' she gasped.

The urgency of the moment left her no time. Throwing the sack to one side, she sifted through the artefacts on the ground, pulled out a tobacco tin and prised it open. She spread the map out on the ground and took the trowel out of her rucksack.

'Come on, come on,' she whispered to herself, gathering up the chimes, bells and ankle bracelets and dropping them in her rucksack. She rushed along the wall to the edge of the old factory floor. The rusty cauldrons, once used to boil the sugar when the factory was alive, had disappeared under mounds of earth, and were covered with a carpet of rough grass like the stubble on a man's face. Bending down, she dug into the ground, fishing out another tobacco tin. She cross-checked the map. Over and over again she dug up the artefacts and then bolted back up Sun Street, her bulging rucksack banging painfully on her legs.

When she got back home, she ran out to the yard at the back of the house and fell on her knees, spilling the artefacts on to the grass. Hacking away at the soil, she made a hole and pushed the precious items inside. Desperately, she squashed down the disturbed earth and dragged a potted banana tree over the top.

Exhausted, she pulled herself up and disappeared into the house to wash the traces of dirt from her hands.

*

The next day, Laxmi was plaiting her hair when the sound of the reporter's voice on the television distracted her. Turning up the volume, she leaned so close to the screen it nearly touched her nose.

'This tin ticket you see here today is an important find in the history of our island,' he said, pointing to a glass cabinet in a dimmed room. 'This single item, found in the shadows of a chimney stack in Belle Mar, is one of a rare collection of identity tags worn by labourers from India more than a hundred and fifty years ago. The identity of its owner remains a mystery, for now at least.'

'Forever,' said Laxmi, twisting a black band around each plait.

Placing her rucksack on the table, she reached inside, running her fingers along the rough edges of the trowel. She lightly rummaged around again and pulled out one of the tobacco tins she had dug up the day before. Gently, she prised the lid open. Inside was a sheet of paper that had been folded in half then rolled up into a scroll no bigger than a grown man's thumb. Unravelling it, she ran her finger along the central fold so as not to tear the delicate paper - much as her mother had done to the photograph of Laxmi's grandfather. It was her great-grandmother's contract. She had slipped it out of the tin ticket the day before, when the reporter was busy greeting Mr Gopal at the old sugar mill.

The clicking of heels cut through Laxmi's warm glow of self-satisfaction.

'I'm coming, Anju!' she yelled, closing up the tobacco tin and slipping it back in her rucksack. She switched off the TV, took a final glance through the window at the banana tree, and stepped out into the sunshine.

For today, at least, Sun Street was living up to its name.

AFTERWORD

When I was growing up in North London, there was a velveteen map of Guyana hanging on the wall in our dining room. It was a fascinating map in the shape of a long scroll, about a foot and a half wide, and on it were several major landmarks in the country such as the Kaieteur Falls, gold and bauxite mines, and Demerara - where the famous Demerara sugar originated. You have probably tasted the distinct caramel-coloured, toffee-flavoured crystals in your coffee or baked your favourite cake with it without knowing its incredible history. It was the source of many a dinner-table conversation in our house during my childhood, when we children heard about, and tried to understand, the links between our family and one of the most controversial commodities in the world.

My younger siblings and I, who were all born in London, were told fantastic stories of water canals and crocodiles, cane fields and cricket - perhaps to cover up the darker stories of rural poverty and discrimination brought about by years of colonial rule.

Growing up, I became fascinated by the experiences of Indians in Guyana and their links to the sugar trade in the mid-nineteenth century. In 2013 I launched the Social History Hub, an online not-for-profit organisation created to enable ordinary people to share their memories. I saw it as a way of ensuring that their achievements were recorded for future generations. In addition, I set up a page dedicated to 1838 – the year when the first ships carrying indentured labourers for sugar-cane plantations left India for the Caribbean region. This was intended to encourage and collect personal memories of Indo-Caribbean people.

In a series of podcasts, I recorded the views of Londoners who had achieved extraordinary things in their lives. Then, in 2015, I explored my heritage and the history and legacy of Indian migration in *Sugar, Saris and Green Bananas*, a two-part radio series broadcast on BBC Radio 4. It triggered a new interest as I became intrigued by the wider Indian diaspora - those who had migrated, as my own ancestors had done, to other parts of the British Empire. The documentaries, produced by the founder of Culture Wise Productions, Mukti Jain Campion, had excellent reviews in the mainstream press.

That is how the idea for this collection began to grow. I approached Arts Council England to fund the project. I intended not only to explore the history of the indenture programme as a series of fictional short stories, but also to inspire others to explore their own heritage and use their personal archive of photographs, letters and memories to write about their own experiences.

In the first instance, I met with the writers' development organisation called Spread the Word, as well as asking staff at the British Library - which is home to a vast collection of India Office archive material - for their support. I made contact with the author Jamie Rhodes, whose own collection, *Dead Men's Teeth*, used historical archives to create new fiction. Clem Seecharan, Emeritus Professor of Caribbean History and author of several books on Indo-Caribbean history, came on board too. I soon found that I had a brilliant team of people willing me on to make this project a success. Only then did I approach Rosemarie Hudson, Managing Director of HopeRoad Publishing, and was delighted when she agreed to publish my stories.

I decided to write *Sugar, Sugar* because of the absence of first-hand experiences of Indian migration from 1838 to 1917. Most of the archive that is available for this period is written from the perspective of the owners of the sugar estates, managers or surgeons.

Their points of view are revealing but largely spoken with one voice: that of the authorities. Driven by the desire for profit, their accounts were often laced with inaccuracies and falsehoods to maintain the status quo. I am grateful to Arts Council England for enabling me to take some time to research and write about this largely unknown aspect of history.

Sugar, Sugar is, however, not just about history but also about legacy. With future generations in mind, I have tried to include age-old themes such as identity and loss, and put them into more contemporary settings. *The Berbice Chair*, *Identity* and *The Dinner Party* are all indicative of this. My hope is that younger readers will pick up this collection and feel a sense of belonging with other communities from the diaspora. I also hope that they will share their stories and record them as I have done. The young academic Reshaad Durgahee has attempted to do this by coining the phrase 'The Indentured Archipelago'. It is an inspired, unifying geographical term from which emerges a collective shared history, influenced by his own Fijian-Indian roots. I like the term, not least because it conjures up wonderful images of tropical landscapes from the Pacific, the Caribbean, Africa and Asia. Like the islands that make up Fiji, I imagine a chain of events linked by one history that changed the lives of over a million Indians.

The migration of Indian workers to the British colonies coincided with the Abolition of Slavery in 1834. For four years, former slaves were compelled to work on the sugar plantations following Emancipation. The British, anxious to maintain the level of sugar production, were soon focusing their attention on India as a new source of labour. They tested the indentured programme in Mauritius in 1834 and in 1838 began recruiting Indian migrant labour in larger numbers. 1838 is the starting point for this collection.

So, after several trips to the British Library and many conversations with family, friends and members of the community, here is *Sugar, Sugar*. I hope that as you read the stories, you will feel inspired to write your own stories in order to record them for future generations.

BIBLIOGRAPHY

Sweetening Bitter Sugar by C. Seecharan (first edition), published by the University of the West Indies Press, Kingston, Jamaica, 2005, p. 52

Old Bee would recline in a 'Berbice' chair with a bell attached to it. He rang it to demand another drink of his servants or to command instant service for the most absurd errand: once installed in his chair, he would do nothing for himself.

*

In Celebration of 150 Years of the Indian Contribution to Trinidad and Tobago edited by Dr Brinsley Samaroo, Dr Kusha Haraksingh, Prof. Ken Ramchand, Gérard Besson, Diane Quentrall-Thomas, published by Historical Publications Ltd, 61 Picton Street, Port-of-Spain, Trinidad, 1995; 'Names and Meaning', pp. 286-88

*

Chutney Village: In Commemoration of Indian Arrival Day 2000 edited by Jim Jinkoo; 'Indo Caribbeans in the UK', p. 9

*

Indian Overseas: A Guide to Source Materials in the India Office Records for the Study of Indian Emigration 1830-1950 by Timothy N. Thomas, published by the British Library, London, 1985, *https://www.bl.uk/reshelp/pdfs/indiansoverseas.pdf*

*

Indian Diaspora: Socio-Cultural and Religious Worlds edited by P. Pratap Kumar, published by Brill Publishers, Leiden, 2015; 'The World Becomes Stranger, the Pattern More Complicated: Culture, Identity and the Indo-Fijian Experience' by Brij V. Lal

*

Turn North at the Tombstone by Walter Gill, published by Hale, London, 1970

*

Essays on Indentured Indians in Natal edited by Surendra Bhana, published by Peepal Tree Press, Leeds, 1990

*

Sorgho and Impee, The Chinese and African Sugar Canes, Sugar and Sugar Making by Henry S. Olcott, published by A. O. Moore, Agricultural Book Publisher, 1858, *https://archive.org/details/sorghoimpheechin00olcoiala*

*

The Journal of Pacific History, Vol. 39, No. 3, published by Taylor & Francis, 1999; 'Bound for the Colonies: A View of Indian Indentured Emigration in 1905' by Brij V. Lal, *https://www.jstor.org/stable/25169453?seq=1# page_scan_tab_contents*

*

The Indentured Archipelego, a film by Reshaad Durgahee, *https://mediaspace.nottingham.ac.uk/media/t/1_pcrxzs9v*

*

Additional reading

National Archives: *https://sharresearch.files.wordpress.com/2011/07/indian-indentured-labour.pdf*

Vintage Mauritius: *http://vintagemauritius.org/discover/old-chimneys-of-mauritius/*

L'Aventure du Sucre: *http://www.aventuredusucre.com/en*

ACKNOWLEDGEMENTS

So many people helped to get this collection of short stories to you and I am grateful for their encouragement and support.

Rosemarie Hudson, my publisher who understood my passion and gently nudged me to the finishing line; Eva Lewin, Writer Development Manager from Spread the Word for her constant support; Jamie Rhodes, my excellent mentor whose infectious love of writing spurred me on; Prof. Clem Seecharan, whose historical perspectives and anecdotes were delivered with such passion; Mireille Fauchon for her beautiful illustrations and encouraging words; Sarah Sanders from Arts Council England for supporting the project; Nur Sobers-Khan and Emma Morgan at the British Library for helping me to unlock some exciting archives; Suresh Rambaran for sharing his wonderful stories; Reshaad Durgahee for filling my head with Fijian archives; Trimbuk and Sneh for their memories of Durban; Joan Deitch, my copy-editor; Naina and Poonam, my dear friends who lifted my spirits; Aunty May and Uncle Joe for keeping the legacy alive with precious stories from Guyana; Anthony, my brother, and sisters Meg and Sarah for always being there; Raj, my husband for handling the disruption to our lives so patiently; and my daughters Shakira and Tanisha for their young critical eyes and their enduring faith in me - and endless cups of tea.